"This is bad, Skye. You understand?"

Warren was obviously under great strain. "Guy's been waiting for this opportunity for years. He'll use it to ruin us."

"But it's family business!" she protested. "Can't we settle it among ourselves?"

"I don't think we can, because Guy won't let us."

"Oh—no." Skye sat powerless, visualizing Guy's forbidding face. The Reardon time had come, and there was no question that all the Reardons were extremely bitter.

"You're the only one who could get to him," Warren was saying with a feverish intensity. "You're the only Maitland he cares for—he'd destroy the rest of us in minutes. I swear to you, Skye. I know Guy is ruthless. He thinks his father is dead because of us."

Almost a Stranger

Margaret Way

Harlequin Books

TORONTO • NEW YORK • LONDON
AMSTERDAM • PARIS • SYDNEY • HAMBURG
STOCKHOLM • ATHENS • TOKYO • MILAN

Original hardcover edition published in 1984
by Mills & Boon Limited

ISBN 0-373-02634-X

Harlequin Romance first edition July 1984

CHAPTER ONE

ALL the cars had gone and now she and Jeremy stood alone in the garden her father had created out of nothing and turned into the showpiece the whole neighbourhood took pride in. The roses were out in abundance; pink and gold and crimson, all tints in between, and Skye thought she would never again smell their glorious, heady fragrance without experiencing heartbreak or remembering the terrible desolation of this day.

Above them, ironically, instead of weeping, the sky was a cloudless, intense blue and the jacarandas in magnificent full bloom were so breathtaking that a passing car slowed down dramatically while the driver and his passengers stared out transfixed.

'Poor darling!' Jeremy drew her aching head against his breast. 'My poor, poor little girl!'

It was true; she felt as lost and abandoned as a small child. Skye closed her eyes. She understood that Jeremy loved her, but it didn't seem to matter. Nothing mattered anymore.

'I hate to leave you,' Jeremy murmured into her hair.

But clearly he was going to. Skye made a tremendous effort and drew away. Her tears were still wet against her cheeks and her pallor very pronounced.

'Why today of all days do I have to be in court?' Jeremy asked the heedless sky. 'Promise me you'll go inside and lie down.'

'I'll be fine, truly. You go.' Her voice didn't sound like her own, but raw from weeping.

'Surely Fiona or Kathy could have stayed with you?' Jeremy demanded disapprovingly.

'They wanted to, but they have jobs as well,' Skye reminded him remotely. 'Besides, I'd like to be alone. One *is* so terribly alone, you know—past consolation or sharing. That's the terrible part.'

Jeremy stiffened, then pecked distressed little kisses all over her face. 'But, darling, you're not alone. You have me. I know you and your father were very close, but can't you see you have me now to turn to? I love you—I loved you the first time I saw you, I love you now, I'll love you always.'

His earnestness was undeniable. 'Dear Jeremy,' Skye murmured automatically. 'You'd better go now, you'll be late.'

'I will.' A troubled little exclamation broke from him. Jeremy was only a junior member of a prestigious law firm and in no position to take risks. 'You're so white, I'm afraid you might faint.'

She just looked at him with her great violet eyes brilliant with pain. 'I've never fainted in my life.'

'You mustn't!' he urged her, and thrust her head against him again. 'Be brave, darling, and I'll be back just as soon as I can. Just you and me together.'

And if that was meant to comfort her, it didn't.

Skye walked with him to his car while Jeremy protested yet again that he really wanted to take her over to stay with his mother.

'She's very fond of you, as you know.'

Skye couldn't even summon up the strength to deny it, or shudder at Mrs Phillips parting words of comfort, '*lovely* funeral!' Just the thing to say to a mourning daughter, however sincerely it was meant. Maybe later she might shriek. It could hit her later. People had been known to go into gales of laughter at funerals, even the most deeply bereft.

Jeremy kissed her goodbye again and just as she thought it might go on indefinitely, he folded his slim, elegant body into the driving seat and leaned across to issue a brisk order.

'Take a few tablets and lie down, darling. Life is frightful for you at the moment, I know, but your father wouldn't want you to make yourself ill with grief.'

His bracing manner reminded Skye irresistibly of his stylish, slightly alarming mother. 'At least I can spare him the day!' Skye exclaimed with a manic return to her old tartness. She knew Jeremy was genuinely concerned for her, but it was quite obvious he didn't want her to spend too much time mourning the father she had adored. Good-looking, ambitious, with what his mother called, 'winning ways', Jeremy had let it be known very early in their twelve-month relationship that he considered her too attached to her father.

'Special circumstances, darling, I know, but you should realise you're going to have to break the parental bond.'

Jeremy, too, lived at home, but obviously he didn't see it posed the same sort of problems.

Skye stood watching as Jeremy's silver Volvo moved sedately off, then stopped altogether as the Williams' dog dashed on to the road, then she turned and walked back along the stone pathway, her eyes shining with unshed tears. She had always thought of herself as a spirited sort of girl, indeed Jeremy's mother often expressed jovial disapproval of Skye's spirited ways and opinions (what woman is *really* interested in politics?), but now she felt absolutely terrified of being alone. Only two terrible weeks since her father had suffered his fatal heart attack, and the pain of loss, the unalterable shock of it was enormous.

How could she ever begin to accept that he had gone? How could she ever begin to let go? Theirs had been a powerful attachment, constructed of their loving natures and the particular circumstances of their lives. Jeremy's carefully veiled resentments had been rooted in jealousy, and it was true that her father, while liking Jeremy, had not regarded him highly. Skye had become increasingly sure of that, although her father had never interfered but allowed her to make her own friends and form her own judgments.

The front door stood open, but Skye couldn't bear to walk inside. The house they both had loved seemed suddenly quite empty—so much so that she would have to move away. Her father would want her to pick up her life, gain control. And to do that she would have to leave her painful memories behind. Even this garden, dazzling in its spring-into-summer display, she found unbearable. The old enchantment was gone. The flowers, the myriad scents, only added to her pain. Nevertheless she moved to the stone garden seat and sank down in exhaustion. Always a very slender girl, she had lost many pounds in weight and she realised vaguely that she was looking very frail. Of course she wasn't eating; that was too much to expect. No more shared meals, no more friends over, no more impulsive dining out. Not a sick day in his whole life, yet her father had died almost at once. No power on earth could rouse her from her misery.

A few moments later she was faintly chilled to realise that the man in the large limousine parked a little distance along the road had been observing her for some time. She had an absurd impulse to pick up a stone and hurl it at the gleaming car; her natural volatility at war with her enforced stupor. Her face must have registered her distressed anger, because the man got out of the car and began to move towards her.

She had seen him before—that outline, very tall and lean, broad-shouldered. Images slipped in and out of her mind. He was sombrely, impeccably tailored, and Skye suddenly remembered he had been at the service. She had been dimly aware of an unfamiliar presence and thought it someone from the University where her father had been a lecturer. Now, her face flushed with aversion, she saw it was someone from another world—her grandfather's world. The aura was unmistakable.

Skye stood up and deep inside her an elemental antagonism flared up, overwhelming grief and pain, proving that ultimately the living were thrust forward by the surge of events. Anger countered her bodily weakness and by the time the man reached her, her peculiar pallor had faded and she was able to speak in her clearest, crispest voice.

'Surely you've been studying me for some time?'

'Miss Farrell?' His voice was as clipped, as diamond-sharp as her own.

'*Please!*' Contempt flashed from her striking eyes. 'You know perfectly well who I am. You were at the funeral, weren't you?'

He nodded his dark head. 'I was. I've delayed the opportunity to speak to you until now.'

'Very wise.'

His eyes were a frosted grey or a cool grey with a dangerous gleam in them. 'Guy Reardon, Miss Farrell. I'm here on behalf of your grandfather, Sir Charles Maitland.'

She had known it, of course. That was why she cried out in merry bitterness. 'My grandfather? How nice. And how is Sir Charles?'

'Deeply concerned about you.'

'Bunkum!' To her horror she found she was shaking with anger. 'He didn't even know he had a granddaughter until now!'

'It was an extremely difficult situation,' he assured her, his face, except for his eyes, an expressionless mask. Tension laced the air, far headier than the overwhelming scent of the roses.

'A situation that my father won,' Skye reminded him with heavy irony. 'I don't know how he beat my grandfather, but he damned well did!'

'Can't you forget all that?' he asked quietly. 'Leave it in the past?'

'Oh, *please*!' She took an involuntary step forward, staring up at him, 'Aren't you and my grandfather expecting a bit too much? From the look of you I guess you're used to twisting women around your little finger, but not me. If you have to report back to my grandfather, that's your problem. He has no meaning for me. For twenty-two years of my life he was glad to forget I existed. Now the very day my father is buried, he's going to get you to convince me he's a human being!'

'You're very bitter, aren't you?' he said harshly.

'That's for sure.' She swung her hair back, frightened by the antagonism and attraction this man stirred up.

'Won't you please come out of this hot sun and just listen to what I have to say?' he begged her.

'There's nothing we could possibly talk about, Mr Reardon. My grandfather really *is* the ogre I think he is. I see no reason why we should pretend that he isn't.'

'I see.' There was a dark brooding in his expression. 'You're not interested in hearing his side of the story?'

'I've *heard* his side of the story!' Skye exploded, and as she did so, her head seemed to leave her shoulders.

He moved so quickly he must have had the premonition she might faint. His arms were locked around her and he was tilting her head down, his hand locked firmly around her nape.

'Breathe deeply, Skye,' he said.

She felt like a small child in the competent, experienced hands of an adult. Even with the world whirling she had to concede the intolerable, easy authority.

'Better now?' he asked.

'Great!'

'You could make life hell for yourself, little one, if you don't just calm down.'

She felt too weak to argue with him, all her energies burnt out.

He didn't even hesitate. There was no choice. He swung her into his arms and regardless of the shock and the inevitable helpless anger that assailed her, carried her into the house.

'Oh, *thank* you!' she said tightly as he lowered her full length on to a sofa.

'Any brandy in the house?' He looked around him, then unerringly went to the richly decorated Chinese cabinet that housed a small selection of spirits and liqueurs.

'I don't drink,' Skye moaned a little.

'Thank God for that! I suspect in your cups you might go up in smoke.'

Their fingers touched when he handed her the crystal glass, and it was too much for her. There seemed to be fire in the contact, or *she* was on fire.

'Slowly,' he said easily as she seemed on the verge of tossing it off.

'If I drank it slowly I wouldn't be able to drink it at all.' The liquid coursed down her throat in a gentle fireline and she gasped and felt stronger all at the same time.

'I suspect one could get used to that,' she said.

'Lie back a moment,' Guy Reardon pushed her gently into the mound of silk pillows.

'I never realised you'd be so much like your mother.' His silvery eyes narrowed over her; over her face, her hair, her breasts, her long, slender legs, and it seemed impossible, but she trembled under a man's regard.

'You couldn't possibly remember my mother, Mr Reardon,' she countered bluntly. Although everything about him exuded consequence, he couldn't have been more than thirty-three or four.

'On the contrary,' for the very first time he smiled at her, 'I've retained her image very well. As a small boy I thought her the most beautiful creature I'd ever seen. Actually, I think, it was the first time I fell in love.'

'Charming! How charming!' The mockery was a defence against the devastation of that smile. 'From the way you say it, it's happened many times since?'

'Daily, hourly, until I was into my twenties.' He drew up an armchair and sat near her, his magnetism so strong she thought she should be able to see and touch it. 'You're looking a little better. *Are* you?'

'I'm going to tell you something in strictest confidence,' she took a deep breath. 'I feel threatened.'

'You're not showing it.'

'I'm making a point of not letting it show, but I feel . . . endangered, all the same.'

'Can you tell me why?' He gave her a brittle smile.

'As though my entire world is about to change. *Has* changed.' Her delicate nostrils dilated and tears filled her eyes. She turned her head away and her luxuriant hair spilled over the cushions, red like a flame against the apple green silk.

She heard him say her name gently and she bit hard on her lower lip.

'There'll be peace in your world again, Skye. Joy *and* justice.'

'Justice? What's that? Let me tell you it wasn't easy for my father. He had quite a struggle rearing a daughter from infancy—*alone*. My grandfather, even then, was a rich and powerful man, a very callous man. He drove his only daughter away and then when she died he sought to take all my father had left. The miracle was that he couldn't convince the judge that my father was the unfit guardian he made him out to be.'

'Even the most intelligent, reasonable people can be blinded by their emotions, Skye,' Guy Reardon told her. 'Your grandfather suffered greatly when your mother died. He idolised her, you know.'

'There must be a bit more to *idolising* than throwing

your daughter out when she makes what appears to be an unsatisfactory marriage?'

'So you *do* see your grandfather could have been alarmed at your parents' hasty marriage. They were very young.'

'Old enough to choose which way they wanted to go.'

'Wait until you're a parent, Skye,' he told her. 'If you are, don't think you're going to miss out on a lot of upsets.'

'You, on the other hand, are too wise, too reasoned, ever to make a mistake?'

'We're not talking about me, my future,' his vibrant voice was edged with steel. 'Instead of bitterness, can't we talk of reconciliation? If you wanted your grandfather punished, he *has* been punished—many times over. You're certainly not the right one to judge. I would say he has wanted you from the day he held his dying daughter in his arms. I can't deny that his grief turned to hatred. It's common knowledge that he did blame your father for your mother's tragic, early death. Anguish takes people in many ways.'

'What about guilt?' Skye swung up half-way to defend her father. 'Wasn't it guilt that made him hate my father?'

'Maybe both of them had only their violent passions to sustain them. Can't there be an end to it?'

'Today of all days? My God!' She stared past him and her violet eyes shone with tears. 'I don't really hate my grandfather, Mr Reardon,' she began to struggle for breath, 'but you must forgive me if I can't love him either. Tell him I forgive him if he needs my forgiveness to survive, but I don't feel anything could be achieved by my meeting him. My father is dead. It's all over.'

'Don't, Skye!' he begged.

Her heart seemed to twist at her name on his lips. 'Oh yes, I can. Haven't you heard of natural justice?'

'Only you're a generous person, aren't you? Your grandfather meant no cruelty to you. I respect and admire what he's now trying to do.'

'Why not?' she taunted him bitterly, longing all of a sudden to hurt him as he was hurting her. 'You're like him, aren't you? I despise and fear the qualities in both of you.'

'And you can see them, can you? You're perfectly comfortable with your judgments.'

'I know not to trust you, Mr Reardon. I remind myself that you're my grandfather's man.'

Something flickered in his shimmering eyes, 'I'm my own man. I have to be,' he said with dangerous pleasantness. 'I wanted to do this for your grandfather.'

'Whatever for?' Points of colour stood out on her cheeks.

He learned forward. 'Why not? Our families are tied. Your cousin Warren is to marry my sister.'

'The marriage of the year, is it?' Skye lay back exhausted, veiled intensity in every line of her body.

'*They* think so.' The dark, determined face was lit by that smile again.

'I'm sorry,' she looked away. 'I don't know my cousin Warren or your sister, though I'm sure they're far from ordinary. As a matter of fact I've never even received a scrap of paper from my cousins with just a simple, "Hello there!" '

'You wrote to them a lot?'

'Surely I was the one in the embarrassing situation?' she pointed out.

'I suspect your cousins, Skye, like you, did what they were told,' said Guy Reardon.

'What's a cousin more or less?' There was derision in her blue lotus eyes. She put her feet to the floor deliberately, then stood up. 'Is there anything else, Mr Reardon, you wanted to ask of me?'

'Yes. Don't wreck your life.'

'My life, Mr Reardon,' she said, her voice rising, 'is *my* business. I can see exactly why you want to please my grandfather, but you can't treat me like a piece of office furniture. Your coming here was all a waste of time. Life is senseless and rotten. The good people die and the. . . .'

He reached for her. He just reached for her quite naturally and drew her into his arms. 'Quiet, Skye, I can hear you.'

It was like being at the centre of some violent storm while all within the eye was quiet, but a movement forward or backwards could precipitate a great crisis. How could this man comfort her? She thought there was no one left in the world capable of it, yet this strange physical intimacy, his arms locked around her slender body, were taking something from her he had no right to.

'I'm very sorry about your father,' he said above her. 'I know what it's like to lose a beloved parent, the whole appalling pain of severance. My own father played an enormous role in my life. Everyone said to me, 'give it time,' and that's all I can say to you, Skye. Give it time. And give some thought to a reconciliation with your grandfather. I'm telling you the real truth about how he feels. Look at me.'

Too spent to do anything else, she lifted her head, appalled now to find she was paralysed by his closeness. He knew it too. She saw just the flash of it in his eyes, then he released her like the only possible move he could make.

'Your grandfather has never for a single day forgotten your existence,' he assured her. 'There are many things I could tell you, but I know you don't want to hear them now. All I can do is urge you to respond to your grandfather's overture. You need him.'

'I *don't*.'

'And he needs you.'

'I can't even begin to comprehend why.' Skye put a hand to her throbbing head. 'There's an old saying, Mr Reardon, I'm sure you've heard of it—let sleeping dogs lie.'

'Your grandfather knows he owes you a great deal.'

'Then let him write me a cheque. No ridiculous sum, just a token—and while he's about it he can sit down and write you one as well. You're very persuasive.'

'And at another time,' he said neatly, 'I'd be pleased to turn you over my knee. Right now I think you need a good square meal.'

'I shall attend to it immediately you've gone.'

'Only I'm guessing you have very little in the house. That's the way it is when you feel utterly alone.'

'I . . . I. . . .' She wanted to throw him out, but she couldn't.

'At least allow me to take you out for a quiet meal,' he said. 'I'm sure you haven't eaten properly in days.'

'Weeks!' she exclaimed in wry despair. 'If I do, Mr Reardon, would you please go away afterwards? I can't fight you or argue. I can't trust you either, though I realise you're a clever and sophisticated man. I'm going to get through my life, and I hope to God I never hear from my grandfather again. It's too late.'

He chose a riverside restaurant perched up on a cliff, and the proprietor took one look at him, then guided them personally to a secluded table that commanded the best view.

Skye sat down in the chair that was pulled out for her, not caring if she looked as woebegone as she felt. She had changed her black dress for a blue silk, run a brush through her full, springy mane of hair, then launched herself back into the living room where Guy Reardon had looked at her with an expression that was disquieting and compassionate at once. Now in this restaurant she felt utterly unreal, forced into a strange intimacy with a stranger. And he *was* a stranger. She couldn't understand how he seemed so startlingly familiar. Or how so smoothly he had taken charge.

'Is there anything you don't care for, Skye?' he asked her.

'Not really.' She looked down at her folded hands.

'Then I'll order for you, shall I?'

'All right.'

He lifted his hand and the hovering maître d' moved swiftly to take his order. Their waiter appeared. Some people, Skye thought wearily, were born to be deferred to. Once she and her father had visited this restaurant, and she couldn't help remembering that though the service had been quick and pleasant they hadn't received this kind of attention. The power brokers had some mysterious force field of their own. It worked across crowded rooms and people responded like robots programmed to obey. She couldn't think why she hadn't put up a better struggle herself. Probably when her grandfather had sent him, he knew Guy Reardon was the right man for the job.

All through the meal he murmured weightless pleasantries, pushing plates, glasses and even her knife and fork into a more inviting position. Everything was absolutely delicious with a superb aroma, but so far as Skye was concerned it was difficult to taste it. The enormity of the day held her locked in its strain, her violet eyes enormous, her flawless skin very white. She looked what she felt, hideously vulnerable and alone.

At last she felt she could safely set down her knife and fork. 'There you are. I hope I didn't disappoint you, but no more.'

'No more,' he agreed quietly. 'Coffee, though, surely?'

'Coffee, of course.' She raised her head and the shining mass of her hair flooded her shoulders. 'May I ask you a few questions?'

'How many?' he smiled at her, surprisingly sweet and vivid in so formidable a face.

'Did you think I would fall in with my grandfather's plan?'

'You haven't even heard his plan,' he pointed out mildly.

'Oh, you know, it doesn't really matter.'

'Whatever the bitterness and pain of the past,' he reached out and touched the tips of her long, slender fingers, 'you can be sure your grandfather wants to make it up to you.'

'Money?' Just for a moment Skye allowed her fingers to rest unresistant under his.

'Don't you like money?' he queried.

'Certainly I do—my *own*. Earning it gives me a great satisfaction.'

'You work for James Hendersen, don't you?'

'Well done!' Whether she had wanted a meal or not it made her feel remarkably stronger. 'Is there anybody you don't know?'

'Hendersen is still a young man, to be so successful.'

'The important thing is knowing where you want to go and having the ability to get there,' Skye pointed out.

'Plus a lot of luck.'

'Luck?' Suddenly she searched his face with those sizzling, frosty grey eyes. 'I'm quite certain you became important to my grandfather with no luck at all.'

He returned her challenging gaze very steadily as befitting his dignity. 'There was a time when my family and your grandfather were very much at war. It's obvious you don't know much about big business in this country, or you might have heard about it.'

'Why don't you tell me?'

He put his wine glass down. 'Because you don't really want to hear. And because you are who you are. That way if I ever decide to give your family the coup de grâce you won't know about it.'

'On the contrary,' she said triumphantly, 'I think it

would do them good. I have an uncle and two cousins,
I understand?'

'They live with your grandfather,' he nodded his
head. 'Your uncle Justin, his wife Felicity and Warren
and Jo Anne.'

'My God!' Skye twirled her empty glass by its stem.
'And not a one of them to make the slightest attempt
to see me?'

'Remember there was your father, Skye,' he told her
sombrely. 'He must have sent back a million presents.'

'Is that so?' She sank her small white teeth in her
bottom lip. 'I don't believe you.'

'So what? It's true.'

She gave him a look of contempt. 'So we have a
million unopened presents, what else?'

'Total aggression on your father's side. He vowed
he would never speak another word to your
grandfather again and he refused point blank any
family contact with you.'

'And I understand perfectly,' said Skye. 'You didn't
know my father.' Her cheeks were flushed now and
she looked very young.

'I have heard that he was a fine man and highly
respected in academic circles. I have also heard that he
was very, very lonely.'

'Not with *me*.' She trembled.

'I know you were the most precious thing in his life,
Skye, but some people love so deeply, when they lose
a beloved partner they never truly come back to this
world again. When my own father died, my mother
lost every vestige of her old exuberance. That was five
years ago. She's recovered, of course, but I never,
ever, expect to see her shine with joy again.'

'She will,' Skey said unexpectedly. 'She can't as yet
have embraced her first grandchild.'

She hadn't intended to, yet she made his eyes blaze.
'Am I right?' she asked almost humbly.

'Yes,' he said finally.

'You're not married?'

'No.'

'That was very downright,' she commented.

'Indeed it is,' he assured her briskly. 'I thought very highly of my parents' marriage, but not too many since.'

'Oh? What about your sister and my cousin Warren?'

'Your grandfather is delighted to welcome her into the family.'

'I expect she'll have lots to do to justify her existence, but what about you?'

'The usual.' He smiled again, charmingly. 'I hope they'll be very happy.'

'And for yourself? You don't plan to take a wife?'

'This conversation is getting too serious for my liking.'

She gave him a sharp little look upwards. 'Eventually I'm sure some exquisite creature will win your confidence. No serious tycoon can be without an heir. And if *you* don't deliver the coup de grâce, your son can keep trying.'

'More or less,' he agreed very dryly. 'I've always known redheads have very sharp tongues.'

She lifted a delicate shoulder indifferently. 'Well, it doesn't matter, does it? After today it's unlikely we'll see one another again.'

'I think we will,' he said smoothly. 'I knew that from the first. I also knew you'd be very upset and angry but if you allow yourself, you'll get over it. It would be a great pity to allow this vendetta to go on. Your grandfather isn't the towering figure he was, he's tiring.'

'And you're very strong and too wide awake.'

'You catch on very fast.'

She nodded her head bleakly. 'I've always found it useful in my job.'

'You must be very bright.'

'Oh no!' she looked up at him. 'You *haven't* checked with James?'

'I've done nothing that could possibly worry you.'

'You've spoken to James,' she said bleakly. 'Perhaps you've applied some pressure on him.'

'Nonsense.' The dark, vibrant voice was almost curt. 'I have met Hendersen several times, as it happens. He's nice and friendly—*and* tough. I've spoken to him about all kinds of things, but there was no need to speak to him about you.'

'Thank you,' she said flatly. 'You've put me very properly in my place.'

'Actually he needed no encouragement to speak about *you*,' he told her.

'I beg your pardon?' Skye blinked her shock.

'He's quite certain you get your ability from your grandfather.'

Skye knew perfectly well what she meant to do. She stood up, grasped her handbag and stared down at him, her voice low, but perfectly clear.

'Thank you very much for the luncheon, Mr Reardon. I'm not going to thank you *too* much, because it's easily written off as expenses. I don't like being spied on and I don't like being treated like a dimwit who can be manipulated at will. Please tell my grandfather there's nothing he can do for me now. No hard feelings, but that's the way it is. The most important years of my life, he ignored me, so he can't expect to work up a close relationship now. And while you're at it,' she stared down at him, breathing hard, 'you might warn him to look out for *you*!'

The full force of her overwrought state had her whirling, almost careering into a waiter who was sidling like a flamenco dancer through the tables.

'Sorry—I'm sorry!' She felt like a terrified school girl with some menacing figure coming after her, for she was certain Guy Reardon was moving.

The maître d' moved swiftly, holding open the door,

his eyes lingering on her distraught, haunting beauty. A lovers' quarrel, of course, but one that would soon be made up. Beautiful women, especially redheads, soared to great emotional heights, then plummeted to the depths. In fact, he thought tolerantly, all women fluctuated madly—probably some complexity of the female brain.

If she hadn't been so acutely angry and upset, Skye would never have moved with such frantic heedlessness. She didn't dare to look behind her, neither did she turn her head in more than one direction. The notion that he would catch up with her and bundle her up into his arms was accompanied by a terrible excitement. For some reason she couldn't even begin to handle, Guy Reardon made her feel comforted, assaulted and devastated all in one swoop.

At the same time as a pedestrian shouted, raising the alarm, Skye finally saw the bright, looming shape that had torn into sight. A compact red coupé had come racing around the corner, the young male driver obviously revelling in its handling power, but by the time both he and Skye reacted another tragedy was closing in on them.

Skye's whole body went icy with fright while a sickening paralysis seemed to take command of her limbs. It couldn't be possible she was about to be run down. Was she dreaming all this? It was some grotesque nightmare. She couldn't even scream, her vocal chords weren't working.

From behind a man's powerful arms seized her, almost crushing the life out of her body, and she was being half lifted, half thrown towards the traffic island while the driver of the car fought to manoeuvre his car to safety. He should never have been cornering so fast, but neither should that fool girl have propelled herself off the kerb like a mindless child.

There was an appalling crunch as metal tore into metal. Splinters of glass sprayed everywhere like water droplets from a pounding surf, but Skye's body was almost fully protected by the much heavier, taller body of her rescuer. They both exploded on to the traffic island where they went down, Skye pinned beneath. Pain attacked her everywhere; her head, her shoulders, her elbows and her knees, then whirling dark clouds started to come for her, but as she tried to fight them off they closed over her, rendering her unconscious.

CHAPTER TWO

SHE was lying on a table and a light was shining in her eyes.

'Good. She's coming around,' a voice said.

'Where am I?' At last she knew why people said that.

'At the P.A., dear—lie still. You're all right, don't be frightened.'

'I'm not.' It was true, she wasn't. Not for herself. 'The man who was with me? Where is he?'

'Don't worry about him either. He's getting stitched up.'

'Then he's injured?' Skye tried to sit up.

The Sister was young and pretty, but she was very strong. 'Lie back.' She managed to press Skye back on to the table with little effort. 'Your friend cut an artery, but he's coping very well. What you might expect from a hero!' She gave Skye a smile. 'He'll be fine, but I think Doctor wants to keep him for a while, probably overnight. He lost a lot of blood and he could need a transfusion.'

'Oh, no!'

'Don't cry, dear—*please!*' the Sister begged.

'I'm *not* crying.' Skye lifted her hand, amazed to find there were tears on her cheek.

'Well now?' The double doors swung open, bringing with them a blast of hospital air. 'How is she?'

'Conscious, Doctor.' The Sister turned her head, speaking to the bluff, middle-aged man who had just walked in.

'Mr Reardon, Doctor?' Skye asked. 'Did you attend to him?'

24

'I did.' Now her arm was being held and her pulse checked. 'Like to see him, would you?'

'I would.' But she was trembling so much she didn't think she could get up.

'Then you can,' the Doctor told her cheerfully, 'when you're feeling a little better yourself. Head clearing now, is it?'

'It's aching.'

'So it should be.' A little more severity now. 'You're bruised and concussed, but mercifully, thanks to your Mr Reardon, you're whole of limb and still alive.'

'And the driver of the car?' Skye swallowed on the sudden lump in her throat.

'Maybe hurting in the pocket, but that's all.'

'Thank God!' Sky closed her eyes.

'I don't care to send her off in this condition,' the doctor said over her head. 'Fix her up with a bed—and what about a sedative?'

'I'll attend to it.' The Sister's voice sounded bright and competent. 'Oh, by the way,' she was saying, 'I'd like you to take a look at Mr Turner before you leave.'

Footsteps moved off and Skye lay there, eyes closed, grateful she was still alive.

When she opened her eyes again, Guy Reardon was sitting beside her bed. She had been put into a small private room that was quiet and blessedly free of the pungent odours of antiseptics and medication.

'How are you?' He looked directly into her eyes.

'But you shouldn't be up!' She turned her head along the pillow, intensely aware of him with every fibre of her being.

'Don't look so worried,' he told her, 'I'm fine.'

'But you *can't* be!' she protested, and her eyes dropped to his injured arm. 'Sister said you had stitches, that you might need a transfusion?'

'They've fixed me up and I'm pretty tough.'

'My God, you must be!' She found herself staring at

him, amazed to see he looked just the same except for a faint pallor. He still wore street clothes and a shirt she hadn't seen before—not of the quality of the shirt that would have had to be discarded, but still he looked remarkably elegant.

'Dr Sullivan kindly lent me a shirt,' he glanced down at himself wryly. 'There was no way I was going to get into that hospital gear. Or no way I'm going to stay.'

'What time is it?' Skye finally became aware of her smarting body, although her pounding headache had quickly settled.

'Just after six.' He checked with his expensive watch. 'I'm almost certain we can both go home.'

'Home?' She looked away from him.

'Or if you prefer, I'll take you to my hotel.'

'I'll go home.' She shook her head. The effects of the sedative had worn off and now she was back to reality with all its desperate misery. 'I have to thank you for saving my life.' Slowly she turned her head back to face him.

'What were you thinking about, Skye?' His silvery grey eyes were serious and searching and between his black, winged brows there was a slight frown.

'Not suicide,' she responded swiftly. 'Surely you didn't think that?'

'I didn't know what to think. I haven't had such a bad moment in my life. It was pure horror. That reckless young fool in the car thought so as well. Maybe it will cure him of speeding around the city.'

'He's . . . he's . . . all right?' she faltered as the ready tears stung her eyes.

'I understand so. I wasn't in much condition to ask him. Just as well!'

'I don't know. It was all my fault.' She spoke softly. 'I just felt so angry, so grief-stricken.'

'Just don't do it to me again.' He took her hand. '*Please?*'

'Do you really believe I should see my grandfather?' she asked. 'Now that you've saved my life you owe me the truth.'

'You're crazy if you thought I was going to tell you anything else at any time,' he returned, faintly mercilessly. 'I believe your grandfather has owed you a great deal for a very long time. I can't pretend I wouldn't have acted differently had I been a member of your family, but I can accept that there were great difficulties. Your father, loving you so much and really only having you, might have been frightened the Maitland way of life might have won you over. Life *is* different for the very rich. Your cousin Jo Anne, for instance, has never worked a day in her life, neither has she ever looked at anything she couldn't have.'

'And of course she's looked at *you*,' Skye said bluntly, and he looked back at her long and hard.

'She does think she's attracted to me,' he agreed.

'Is she beautiful?'

'Very attractive, but I can't see her bothering you.' His dark voice was very dry. 'I won't let you bother me either.'

'I would never want to try to,' she assured him.

'Good.' To her shock he leaned forward and kissed her—not on her cheek or her temple, but very briefly on her mouth.

'That made no sense at all,' said Skye, when she was able.

'Of course it didn't, but the last few hours have been unbearable. One feels compelled to kiss children, especially when they're hurt.'

'It would just be a bit too dangerous if I grew up?' she suggested.

'Yes.' His body untensed and his smile came back again, the most disturbing illumination.

'Together, are you?' A voice hailed them and Guy's head swung around.

'Ah, Doctor,' without hesitation he came to his feet.

'You should be resting you know,' Dr Sullivan told him.

'I needed to see this young woman here,' he explained.

'Nothing much wrong with her now, I'd say.' Dr Sullivan approached the bed. 'Headache gone?'

'All but,' Skye couldn't smile, but her eyes were grateful. 'Thank you, Doctor.'

'Keep your eyes about next time you're crossing a road,' he told her. 'Your friend here,' he gave Guy a quick nod, 'mightn't always be around.'

'I will,' Skye assured him.

'All those grazes smarting?' Dr Sullivan asked more softly.

'I'm too fortunate to worry about them.'

'You're young—beautiful skin. You'll heal in a few days.'

'I'd like to speak to you, Dr Sullivan,' said Guy.

'I know,' the doctor chortled triumphantly. 'You want me to discharge you both.'

'You can't keep us,' Guy gave him a quick grin.

'And you want to be alone.' Dr Sullivan threw his head back and laughed. 'One has no fear, has one, when a loved one's life is in danger?'

'You didn't *have* to let him think we were ... involved,' Skye stammered after the Doctor had gone.

'Keep your cool,' Guy told her. 'It would do no one any good to say we were almost complete strangers.'

'Which we are.' Skye looked away from his brilliant, mocking eyes.

'You don't want to get involved with me, little one, either,' he laughed. 'I'm a bold, bad man.'

And it's already too late. Skye spread her hands out on either side of her and went to move her legs off the bed.

'I'll help you,' he said quickly.

'No, I'll manage,' she gave a brittle little laugh. 'I

have enough of a problem coping with the fact that you saved my life.'

'Oh well—you know, I wanted to really.'

'Brute!' she said snappishly, and he waited for no more.

'Easy, Skye. It's the wrong time to get angry.' Gently, very gently, he eased her to her feet. 'Did I do all that, all those bruises?'

'You did most of them,' she said shakily. 'The pavement did the rest.' Abruptly she slipped away from him, seeing how quickly he had dominated her life.

'I'll send a nurse,' he said almost curtly, glancing at her face.

'Okay. The sooner I get out of here, the better.'

They took a taxi back to the house and despite all her protestations of being all right Guy dismissed the taxi and escorted her to the front door. Inside the phone was ringing, but Skye didn't think she could bear to answer it.

'Shall I?' He looked down at her, sensing how she felt.

'What are you going to say, I'm not at home?'

'I'll say you're lying down.'

'I might have to. It seems to be difficult walking.' She seemed to be terribly stiff.

He glanced at her in his acute penetrating way, then walked to the phone, but as soon as he said, 'Hello,' the caller, apparently in some consternation, hung up.

'Probably Jeremy,' Skye murmured without glancing back. She found the sofa in the living room and sank into it. She was too emotionally exhausted to have to explain herself to Jeremy, let alone explain Guy Reardon.

When she turned her head again he was watching her. 'Do you want to talk or do you want to go to bed? I've decided I'm not leaving you on your own.'

'What if I tell you I *need* to be alone?'

'Tell me anything you like.' For the first time he too showed his exhaustion. His skin was darkly tanned, but she realised as he pulled out a chair opposite her that in repose his handsome face showed a hint of strain.

'Would *you* like to go to bed?' she asked cautiously.

'You mean you're going to allow me to stay?' The smile was back in place again.

'If anyone so deeply tanned could be said to be white, you're *white*,' she told him.

'Oh, this is nice—you're *caring* about me, Skye.'

'I never *did* tell you you could call me Skye,' she said crossly.

'I couldn't settle for Miss Farrell. Besides, I've heard about you for so long I really felt I knew you. I know your face and it was breaking my heart.'

She looked at him sadly. 'You *really* remember my mother?'

'If I didn't, which I *do*, I could steal away any time and stare at her portrait. You're almost a perfect replica except for the cleft in your chin. But where your mother looked wonderfully sweet and nice, I've seen you looking awfully fiery.'

'I *have* to be, that's all.'

'You're shivering,' he looked at her quickly. 'Are you cold?'

'A little, strangely.'

'I'll get a rug. Where?'

'There's a mohair on my bed. Down the hall, first door on the right.'

She seemed to have no choice at all. He was right there in her life. The phone rang again just as he was tucking the rug around her.

'Of course that's Jeremy again.' Mockery was instantly visible in his face. 'This time he's going to demand to know exactly who I am and what business have I answering your phone.'

'Then just let it ring,' Skye said oddly.

'My God, and I thought he was the important man in your life!'

'The important man in my life is dead,' Skye said brokenly.

'From what I saw of this Jeremy he loves you.' Guy slid his hand over her hair and walked to the phone. There were a few moments of inaudible murmuring, then he returned. 'That was Jeremy, and I spoke to his mom.'

'You *what*?' she gasped.

His eyes sparkled in his sharply amused face. 'I would say by now they're checking with Interpol, or at least the Federal police.'

'Please be serious.' She held her hand over her heart.

'I *am* serious,' he looked at her ruefully. 'Your young man is deeply concerned about you. He called at the house, only to find you weren't at home, and he's rung anxiously ever since. I shouldn't be surprised if his secretary didn't make a call. Certainly his mother wanted to check me out.'

'Sit down again.' Skye chided herself that despite his manner he had suffered a severe shock and the trauma of injury.

'When did it suddenly dawn on you that you didn't return his affection?' Still he stood above her, trapping her with his eyes.

'Believe me, I *do* return his affection,' she declared.

'And you haven't thought of him all this time?' He sank down rather wearily beside her. 'Hell! It was obvious to a blind man which was the one to do the kissing and which the one to turn the cheek.'

'It didn't bother you, the fact that you were spying?' Skye tilted her head back and sighed softly.

'And what does he do, this Jeremy?' he asked her.

'You mean you don't know?'

He turned his head studying the lovely line of her throat. 'I'm not sure if I want to know even now.'

'He's a solicitor.'

'He's *not*!' He sounded shocked.

'With Strang & Morrison.'

'It was clear he had an enquiring turn of mind. This may be an odd time to ask you, but are your brows and lashes naturally that dark?'

'A puzzle, isn't it?' she agreed. 'Black lashes and red hair?'

'I think it's fascinating. They certainly look real, and I'm very close.'

'I'd say it was clear you're as exhaustd as I am,' said Skye. 'Cutting an artery is really severe.'

'Don't lose sight of the fact either that I've an almighty bump on my head.'

'You have?' Her eyes flew open and she sat up to stare at him. 'You didn't tell me. Where?'

'All of a sudden you're interested!' His silver eyes narrowed into a strange wariness.

Entirely unconsciously she put out her hand. He had very thick, crisp black hair, and a few seconds' searching found the bump.

'Oh, I *am* sorry!' she groaned.

'You're crazy, Skye.' He drew back. 'A couple of times today you came close to slapping my face, yet now you're making me feel almost special in your life.'

'Don't feel so terrible about it.' She dropped her head back on to the sofa. 'To tell the truth, I hated you on sight.'

'Because you've been hurt a lot.'

'I'm not sure. You have a certain aura about you— the same aura my grandfather has about him. A lot of women might find that attractive, but it only affirms what I've always been taught to believe. Tycoons make lousy family men.'

'My dear child, by and large, you're right,' Guy agreed.

Some faint slurring in his voice made her open her

eyes, and as she did so she experienced an intense shock. He had his dark head back, relaxed, his own thick black lashes still on his taut skin and his strong bone structure thrown into sharp relief. Seen so close to, he was startlingly handsome. His skin was very fine, close-grained, his straight nose aristocratic, cheekbones pronounced, chin firm to aggression, the mouth . . . disturbing, chiselled out in bold relief.

'You should have stayed in the hospital,' she said gently.

'You should have stayed by my side at lunch.'

'You can understand how I feel?'

'Yes, I can.' The chiselled mouth curved into a wry grimace. 'In fact, little one, only my understanding prevented me from wanting to give you a slap back.'

'That would have been cruel.' She was almost whispering.

'Come back with me, Skye,' he said suddenly.

'Covered in scrapes and bruises?'

'I have to go to North Queensland. I'll be back in little over a week.'

'Please,' he begged.

She sighed, 'But it's hopeless.'

'Call me Guy,' he ordered.

'Just as I told you, Guy, it's hopeless. Miracles don't happen.'

'They happened today.' His eyes came open and he grasped her hand. 'I'm going to take you back with me if I have to tie you up.'

'Because my grandfather will reward you?'

'*Yes*.' He underscored the word dryly. 'Satisfied? I'm doing this because I expect a reward for favours rendered.'

'What reward would you get?' She was really only rambling. It was a curious feeling having him there beside her, a ridiculous feeling of ease as though they knew everything about one another's lives.

'Oh, Jo Anne if I wanted her.'

'If grandfather has Jo Anne, why should he want another?'

'He can't just leave it alone. Even as a little scrap you must have been the image of your mother. Jo Anne and Warren are Gowers—that's their mother's side of the family. Dark hair and dark eyes. That's the funny thing about redheads, they live on in the memory.'

'Are you sure you feel all right?' Skye leaned forward anxiously, seeing him give an involuntary wince of pain.

'I told you, flower-eyes, I'm tough.'

'Does it hurt much?' she asked tentatively.

'Like the devil.' He gave a deep-throated groan. 'You've had a phenomenal effect on me today, Skye. I even laid myself out all over the pavement.'

'I'm sorry,' she said huskily, 'I just went wild.'

'To say the least! You know, I feel absurdly lightheaded.'

I can tell that by just looking at you,' she said. 'I can't understand how they let you out the way they did.'

'I said lightheaded, not *ill*.'

Her hand seemed to rise of its own will and she touched him gently as if to comfort him. 'You don't have to choose *here* to go to sleep. You really should have gone straight back to your hotel.'

'And leave you on your own?' Guy stretched languidly like a sleek cat. 'I don't think you should be on your own, Skye.'

'Neither of us, of course, seems to be considering my reputation,' Skye observed suddenly.

He looked at her in astonishment, amusement lines bracketed his handsome mouth. 'You mean the neighbours might think I'd seek to force my attentions upon you? Me with a gash in my arm, a lump on my head, not to mention a loss of blood and the fact that you're an innocent young girl with the wish furthest from your mind?'

She didn't think on this day it was possible, but she laughed. 'All of which might be true, but it doesn't seem to influence what people think. Your own people back home might think your staying here extraordinary.'

'Time telescopes with some people,' he glanced at her indulgently, but didn't smile. 'I feel I've known you for ever, Skye. I feel for you as I would for a young . . . cousin.'

'I don't know much about how cousins feel for each other,' she shrugged ironically. 'Have you seen the grazes on my knees?'

'Show me.'

'Well. . . .' She unravelled one slender leg and extended it. 'There!' Meticulously she turned back the hem of her blue skirt.

'God knows they're beautiful legs,' said Guy. 'It's a pity to see them chopped up.'

'They'll heal, quicker than your arm.'

'At least it's put you in a better mood with me.' He dropped hs head back against the sofa again, looking sleepy and relaxed. 'Do you think you could possibly do the gentle, womanly thing and make us a cup of tea? Put a lot of sugar in mine.'

'But of course I will!' She stared at him. 'You *are* all right aren't you?'

'Of course I am, darling.'

As an endearment it was said casually, but Skye thought she had never heard the word before. Her cheeks flushed and her eyes sparkled. 'I've nothing against Skye,' she said with a gentle but definite admonition, 'but you can't call me *darling*.'

'Don't be a little bitch, Skye,' he said mildly. 'You're really rather lucky. The only other woman I call darling is my mother.'

'And now,' she said tartly, 'you're just having me on.'

She was moving rather hazily around the kitchen

when she heard the peal of the front door bell, and her heart gave a sudden lurch. Who could possibly be calling on her? She stared at the electric wall clock for a moment as though it could tell her.

'Are you going to answer that, or am I?' Guy called to her with a general lack of enthusiasm.

'I will.' She could hardly ignore it, especially when the bell was being pressed with a heavy, insistent finger. She half hobbled through the hallway, seeing two outlines through the heavy leadlight door. Jeremy and his mother!

When Skye opened the door Mrs Phillips jumped back so violently she might have been totally unprepared instead of excessively anxious to come in.

'*Skye!*' both voices cried at once.

'Jeremy, Mrs Phillips.'

Jeremy's face was a study. 'You could have spoken to me on the phone,' he cried.

'I'm sure there's some very good reason why Skye didn't,' Mrs Phillips told him deliberately, equally furious.

'Please come in,' said Skye, benumbed and exhausted and underneath it all affronted by the twin expressions of considerable disapproval.

'Skye?'

Of course there was Guy Reardon behind her, pleasant, civilised, his physical presence and aura arresting Jeremy and his mother in their tracks.

'I don't think you met Mr Reardon at the funeral,' Skye explained. 'He was representing my grandfather.'

'Your *grandfather*?' Mrs Phillips obviously couldn't decide whether Skye was telling the truth or not. 'I didn't know you *had* a grandfather, Skye. You never speak of him.'

'Sir Charles Maitland,' said Guy Reardon with a certain cool hauteur. 'You're Jeremy, of course, and this is your mother? How are you, Mrs Phillips, Guy Reardon.'

Jeremy couldn't seem to get his wits together and Mrs Phillips took charge, her voice ringing as she straightened everything out.

'Please, shall we go back into the living room?' Skye said.

'You look terrible!' It was at that exact moment that Jeremy dropped his eyes to Skye's nicely painted elbows and knees. 'Mr Reardon said you were resting; he didn't say you'd had some kind of accident.'

'It doesn't matter.' Skye shrugged almost irritably. This was going to be the most terrible day of all time, and all of a sudden she was possessed by a wave of black hilarity. She only wished her father could have been there. Often he and she had gone wild laughing about this or that situation. They had shared the same sense of humour that was awkward now, to say the least. She didn't know whether she should laugh or cry at Mrs Phillips' expression; a combination of fascination, gratification and the awareness that the man Skye had apparently chosen to lean on was not her Jeremy but a total stranger, and moreover a man who was tall, dark and extravagantly good-looking.

'I was just going to make a cup of tea,' said Skye, looking around her.

'Allow *me*, my dear.' Mrs Phillips turned back to her as if shot. She was a tall, generously proportioned blonde woman with a very mastering manner. 'You look . . . er . . . all in!'

'I've been worried about you,' Jeremy told her with his mother's emphasis.

'I know that, Jeremy,' Skye answered gently, 'but really I'm all right.'

In the kitchen Mrs Phillips took the opportunity to take Skye to task. 'But my dear, what is he *doing* here?' She had taken the precaution of shutting the door, now she was standing in front of it, guarding it.

'He didn't tell you the whole story, Mrs Phillips,' Skye explained. 'Trying to save me from being run over, he ran the risk of being killed himself. Thank God he only sustained a relatively minor injury. His arm was badly gashed with either glass or metal, I don't know, and it severed an artery. Both of us finished up in hospital. We've barely arrived home.'

'Great heavens!' Mrs Phillips frowned and looked at Skye as though she fully appreciated her foolhardy ways. 'As to that, why didn't they detain you both overnight?'

'Mr Reardon doesn't seem to like hospitals, and naturally *I* don't,' Skye said bleakly, her mind flashing jaggedly over terrible, recent scenes.

'Of course not, my dear.' All at once Mrs Phillips slumped down on a chair. 'You know, I can't understand you, Skye. Not at all. You say your grandfather is *Sir Charles Maitland*?'

'Don't let it put you off.' Skye hobbled back to the electric kettle and pressed in the button.

'Is that supposed to be funny?' Mrs Phillips asked in astonishment. 'Sir Charles Maitland is a very distinguished man. Why, I was reading an article on him in the *Bulletin* just the other day.'

'Probably it said yet again what a philanthropist he is.'

'A most impressive record, certainly,' Mrs Phillips agreed. 'I can scarcely credit you're his granddaughter. You've always led such a . . . quiet existence.'

'Good for the development of character. I'm told my cousin Jo-Anne has never done a tap of work in her life.'

'But goodness, dear, she wouldn't need to,' Mrs Phillips took time off to point out the obvious. 'Frankly, if I were wealthy, I'd like to keep my daughter at home.'

So this is what Mrs Pankhurst fought for, Skye thought, and crashed the cups and saucers on the table. Give the boys the best education possible and save the girls for marriage.

'I really must help you,' Mrs Phillips said finally. 'Really my dear, we came over to beg you to make use of our guest room. Clearly you can't be by yourself, and Mr Reardon certainly can't stay here. He's *not* staying, of course?'

'You might remember we have a guest room ourselves?' Skye reminded her.

'Yes, but . . .' Mrs Phillips faltered, 'I expect you're so frazzled, you can't cope with it all.'

She didn't have to cope, as it happened. From a faint torpor Guy Reardon had become distinctly authoritative, even to giving Jeremy a slightly vigorous thump on the back as he left.

'For God's sake!' He stared at Skye for some moments. 'What a parent!'

'She adores him,' Skye pointed out.

'Precisely my point. *You*, she can't make head nor tail of until she remembers you're Sir Charles Maitland's granddaughter.'

'It kind of looks like it,' said Skye.

'Surely you can do better for yourself?' he suggested. 'Why, I know a hundred more eligible young men who would court you with incredulous delight.'

'I don't want to be courted,' she said.

'Tamed, then.' He looked down at her with his brilliant eyes. 'I thought you'd like to know protocol had been observed. I told Mrs Phillips we're all but related.'

'I couldn't hear what you were telling her, you were speaking so low.'

'How about bed?' His hands were on her shoulders.

'I'm just so bonged I might sleep.'

'Well, what about your having the shower first? My skin seems to have quite absorbed the hospital.'

'In fact there are two bathrooms.' Skye slid away from under his hands. 'Plenty of towels. Plenty of everything.' She opened her mouth to say something else, then shut it in case she cried. 'Goodnight, Guy.'

'Tomorrow I go north,' he said.

'With that arm?'

'Certainly with this arm.' His black eyebrows rose. 'I'll get myself out in the morning. I have to be up early.'

'I'll be awake.' Her violet eyes were glazed with sadness. 'There's no sleeping in for me any more.'

In her own bathroom she took a warm, healing shower, put on a fresh nightgown and wrapped herself in her robe, a rather gorgeous thing of Thai silk. It had been the very last present her father had given her, and she had often told him lovingly it was so beautiful she could have very easily worn it to a party.

Her mirror showed her a reflected image. A young girl, average height, too slender, deep red hair springing back from her face and spilling around her shoulders in natural deep waves, large, rather frightened eyes, a full, moulded mouth and a delicately purposeful chin. Tonight her skin was more milk than cream and her violet eyes had a bruised look. 'All in,' Mrs Phillips had said, and it wasn't wide of the mark. She felt battered and unreal, but miraculously the terror had gone out of being alone. She wasn't alone; Guy Reardon was just down the corridor. It was almost impossible to hold on to the fact that he was a complete stranger. Maybe a near brush with death did this to people. She was certain, had Jeremy and his mother not called, they might have gone off to sleep together on the sofa, both of them just that bit off balance.

She realised with some worry that he only had the clothes he stood up in. There were lots of things she could lend him. After her father had bought her this robe she had gone out to buy him the most dashing one she could find. It had been wildly expensive, but it had given her great pleasure. All his life her father had sacrificed for her, and now when she was just beginning to get on her feet and carve out a career, he was gone.

'Mr Reardon?' Skye tapped on the guest room door rather shyly.

'Come in, Skye.' He had obviously thrust into his shirt, for it hung open carelessly to the waist. 'I was just looking at my arm,' he explained.

'Are you going to take those painkillers?' She swallowed a little nervously, never having seen a man so disturbingly masculine.

'I am.' His eyes touched her lightly as though he had no intention of pointing up their intimacy.

'I thought you might like this.' She held out the robe she was cradling. 'I bought it for my father, but he was always waiting for an occasion splendid enough to wear it.'

'Why, thank you, Skye,' he said gently, and took it with the same care with which it was extended.

'He had a more scholarly build than you,' she said quietly, studying the width of his shoulders and the strong wall of his chest, 'but he was tall. Well over si. . . . six . . . f-f-eet.' All of a sudden she crumpled, leaning over like a woman in agony, hugging her fragile body with her two arms.

'My dear. . . .' he muttered concernedly.

She thought she had been all right, immunised by shock. 'Oh, God . . . God!' she wailed.

'*Skye!*' he said urgently.

'I can't bear it. It's *merciless!*' There was desperation in her choking sobs.

'I know. Hard as hell.' With one move he had her in his arms. 'You believe you'll never recover and for a time you won't, but then you'll begin to heal and cherish your memories.'

She didn't answer—she couldn't. She pressed her face to the hard wall of his chest to muffle the sobbing that sounded so wilfully uncontrolled. Her whole body abandoned itself to his comfort, reassured by the steady rhythm of his heart. He was so strong, decisive—an incomprehensible consolation.

'Don't, Skye.' His dark head was bent over her.

'I'm sorry, I can't help it.' Her voice was helpless with self-reproach.

'You sound tortured,' he groaned.

'I'll never see him any more,' she wept.

'Where's your faith?' Guy scolded gently.

'I haven't got any,' she said brokenly. 'I'm past it.'

His grip tightened, penetrating her bones, and Skye laid her hands on his shoulders, lifting her pounding head. 'You must hate this. It's crazy—I don't even know you!'

'Oh?' His eyes had the glitter of diamonds. 'Could you really weep in the arms of *any* stranger?'

'No.' She sounded as though he had trapped her into some merciless confession, staring up at him with drowning eyes. 'But it's still *mad*.'

'You haven't lived enough,' he told her quietly. 'Certain people cut through all barriers, some almost instantly. Others we're indifferent to whether we know them all our lives.'

'And that's the truth.' She gave a jagged little sigh.

'So neither of us planned it.'

'No.'

Only then did Skye realise she was clinging to him, and the knowledge let in a flood of awareness and deep down, too frightful to be acknowledged, the most unbearable physical desire.

'Ready for bed now?' He was looking serious and a little tense.

'Yes.' She let her hands fall. 'Goodnight, Guy. I'm sorry I cried all over you, when you're not feeling terribly fit yourself.'

'I wanted to be here, Skye,' he told her, and for seconds only, touched her mouth with his own.

It was a contact so sweet, so unique, a curious radiance shot right through her body. Skye's lips parted on a yearning gasp, opened like a flower and for a moment she couldn't tolerate his drawing away. The need for comfort drew her on, a feverish imbalance, and even as her brain told her he wanted to withstand her, she was begging for that melting heat.

'*Guy?*'

He could not conceal his tension, but her helpless need was a powerful invocation. Somehow his mouth covered her own again, but exquisitely gently as before but commandingly, taking everything she wanted to offer, while she moved into him, offering a great deal: possession that had never been offered or taken, now an irresistible flame.

'*No!*' He jerked his head away, his voice harsh with self discipline. 'I've got to stop this.'

'I'm sorry.' She felt humiliated beyond belief—on fire, her breasts aching.

'Be still,' he whispered. '*Please!*'

She didn't realise it, but she had been moving against him frantically, moaning with the exquisite pleasure of contact, longing to have her naked skin against his own.

'I want to die.' Now she was trembling violently.

'Do you think I don't want you? Do you think I couldn't take you now?'

'I know I'll be humiliated by this for ever,' she muttered.

'You little fool!' He held her head tightly between his hands as every part of her fought for control. She had read of unbounded desire, rather grateful that she had always managed to keep her own emotions under control; now it had burst upon her like a terrible energy too powerful to contain.

'Why don't you *crush* me?' she said violently.

'Why don't I?' His fingers were like steel against her temples and chin.

'You didn't think I'd be like this when you came to

meet me.' Her oval face was dominated by her great stricken eyes.

'Nothing has happened, Skye,' he said carefully.

'Of course not,' she said bitterly, 'you have the strength to resist me.'

His breath exhaled jaggedly and the strong hands on her face suddenly trembled. 'Do you want me to make love to you?'

'Oh, God!'

'You know you're infinitely off balance?' Guy said quietly.

'I know you hate me and I'm going to hate myself.'

Abruptly the curtness of his tone softened. 'You want comfort, Skye, and I'm here.'

'I don't want comfort,' she said fiercely. If she had thought she did, she was totally convinced now she wanted him. *Only* him, this molten storm. 'You were prepared for everything, weren't you, except the seduction scene?'

'Only you're the most vulnerable little seductress I've ever seen.'

The tenderness was by far the worst, his eyes resting on her as though she was a touching child instead of a woman whose body was throbbing for release.

'Let me go, Guy,' she begged.

'It's difficult to let you go when you're looking so desperate.'

'A few minutes ago,' she said tersely, 'you were looking pretty desperate yourself.'

'Maybe I'm not the strong, silent hero you think I am.' His hands dropped to her shoulders and moved over them. 'It would be so easy to take you to my bed. You're very beautiful Skye, but forgive me, forbiddingly young and defenceless. You should let me kiss you maybe a year from now.'

'*Never!* Never again.' She shrugged her delicate shoulders away from under his hands. 'I hope you won't remember this tomorrow,' she said when she turned at his door.

'Not if you're going to hate it so much.'

'It would always be between us when we meet again.'

'I agree.' His pallor had become very noticeable. 'I've kissed a lot of women, but right now I can't remember their existence.'

'All right, I know you're kind,' she said mercilessly. 'I won't see you off in the morning, Guy. I believe we'd both be a lot happier if we never met again.'

CHAPTER THREE

SKYE slept heavily but badly, her fragmented dreams all filled with disaster and vivid clashes with Guy Reardon, and when she awoke in the morning sunlight was streaming across her bed and the breeze through the open windows was cool and fragrant with the scent of many flowers.

Skye lay on her back and stared at the ceiling, her eyes moving blindly over the lovely mouldings of the plasterwork. For almost all the time she had slept here her eyes had delighted in the soft richness of the ceiling, now she scarcely saw it. She had truly demeaned herself—making a silent offering of her body to a complete stranger!

Unbelievable, frightful. And her humiliation was just beginning. She slid her feet to the floor and pushed the silken strap of her nightdress back up on her shoulder. Her young breasts were revealed and she glanced down at herself with near-horror, frightened now of her own sexuality that had asserted itself so dramatically against all wisdom or caution. She had thought one had to be madly in love to be overcome by desire, yet last night returned to her, flushing her body.

Of course he had gone. The house was quite silent but now something struck her as odd. Her door was open and the small pink boudoir chair was been placed back against the wall. That meant he had entered her room, looked down at her while she was sleeping.

She moaned and her burning memories assailed her again.

'*Stop* it!' She even spoke aloud. Why should she care if Guy Reardon looked down at her sleeping face or as befitting an inveterate seductress she wore nightdresses that were flimsy and almost transparent. She was quite certain he would never come back, though she fully expected another delegation from her grandfather. Had he played her for all she was worth it would have been a brilliant triumph. As it was, if he wanted to, he could blackmail her for ever.

There was a note for her on the kitchen table, terse to the point of tyranny. 'Back some time the 24th. Resolve what you can and let's finish this business.' Bold, black writing, flowing and well formed, a very important, definite GUY.

'We'll see about that!' Skye cried aloud emotionally, the long unremitting depression of bereavement lifting to let in extreme defiance. How dared he think he could order her life no matter whether he had saved it or spared her great harm? *Unfinished business*, was that what she was?

She wanted feedback from James. Being James he had given her the rest of the week off, but now she needed his calm wisdom, and more importantly some inside information about the Maitland business empire and just exactly where Guy Reardon figured in it.

A phone call to James invited her to lunch with him. He hadn't even sounded surprised to hear from her. She could hardly expect him to when he had undoubtedly had a few words with Guy Reardon at the funeral. James respected money and power as much as anyone she knew and eventually he would reach this lofty position himself.

'You're looking very much better,' James told her soothingly when they were left alone at their table.

'Thanks a million, James. I know I look terrible.'

'Dear girl, you could *never* look terrible!' James exclaimed, and gave her one of his choirboy smiles. In his late thirties, James could pass for ten years younger thanks to his fair, attractive looks and his compact, boyish figure. One would have thought him a complete innocent until one looked into his eyes. They were very blue and needle-sharp. Not a penetrating, complex gaze like Guy Reardon, a gaze that wanted to know your heart and your mind and your dreams, but more pragmatic, as though the only big panic was getting rich and leading the good life.

'He's seen you, of course?'

'You might have warned me, James,' she said crossly.

'My dear, since I had nothing to warn you about, I didn't. Reardon and I only passed the merest pleasantries. Of course I realised he'd been sent by your grandfather, but I had no idea what he might say to you. What *did* he say?' James's blue eyes were agog.

'First I want you to tell me a little about Guy Reardon,' said Skye. 'Who *is* he?'

'*La!*' James rolled his eyes. 'I don't know where you've been all your life, but the Reardons were immensely wealthy.'

'*Were?*' she queried.

'Don't get me wrong, they're not going broke, but I think one could say their golden days are over. At least they were thought to have crashed when your grandfather took them over, but I hear a few little things here and there.'

'Such as?' To hide her scrapes and bruises Skye had worn white georgette with long, full sleeves and a tight cuff; now she winced as her right elbow hit the table.

'Something wrong?' James glanced at her in concern.

'I'll tell you later. Go on.'

'You know white is your colour,' James told her. 'Venetian red hair, violet eyes! What a marvellous thing it must be to be a beautiful woman.'

'Would you like to *be* one?' she queried.

'I'd love to.'

'Oh, James,' Skye looked at the laughter in his eyes, 'please tell me about the Reardons.'

'Sure. God knows how you've come this far even with me without knowing something about our top families.'

'It's not as though they live here,' Skye pointed out.

'There was a very big article about your grandfather, let me see . . . a fortnight ago in the *Bulletin*. Was it a fortnight ago? Time spins.'

The waiter towered over them with their drinks.

'Many thanks.' James rewarded him with a large tip.

'I don't want to hear about my grandfather,' Skye said. 'Only about Guy Reardon.'

'Fall in love with him, did you?' James's voice dropped to a conspiratorial murmur. 'One never really knows the truth until it's announced, but I've heard he and Jo Anne Maitland are to make a match of it.'

'You've got that wrong.' Skye knew a great stab of emotion. Emotion she refused to put a name to.

'I don't think so, dear.' James shook his fair head sagely. 'You seem to mind?'

'I heard that my cousin Warren Maitland was to marry Guy's sister.'

'Incestuous, isn't it? All this intermarrying. Yes, I know about *that*, but the deplorable or fascinating fact is, Reardon in a few short years has worked his way to a directorship in all the Maitland companies. It's a jolly miracle at his age, even if he is a Reardon. He didn't come into the organisation on the understanding that he was to go straight to the top. In fact I believe the old man made it very tough for him. The father died, of course. Rather an odd story. For one thing, there was positive enmity between all parties. In fact it was said your grandfather might as well have shot Paul Reardon down. Of course there's no feeling in business, and only the brave and unrelenting succeed.'

'Read ruthless for brave,' Skye said raggedly. 'How did Mr Reardon die?'

'Car crash,' said James in his most enigmatic voice.

'It was a good few years ago. There was some talk of suicide, but the family wouldn't have it. I believe his widow had a breakdown.'

'Yet his son went to work for my grandfather?'

'He couldn't possibly *not*. His family were still major shareholders. From the little I've seen of Reardon,' James said silkily, 'I'd say he's decided to rebuild the Reardon empire and use your grandfather as a stepping stone. A damned sight easier if one marries into the family.'

'You shock me,' Skye said.

'Ducky, you're only a little child.'

'So I've been told.'

'That's how we men like our women, sweet and innocent. Set aside from the ruthless, cut-throat filthy business of making a living.'

'I guess it *is* filthy, too,' said Skye. 'It sickens me sometimes, the way men love power.'

'Women love it too—in their men. Why do you think you see lovely young girls with terrible old men? Money is as big a turn-on as coke. Women mightn't like to make the action, but they like to step pretty close to it. Where was Reardon going?'

Skye went to tell him, then she saw the peculiar glitter in his eyes. 'I've no idea.'

'Now, please—you're protecting him,' James exclaimed.

'*Protecting him*!' She tried a little, disgusted laugh. 'I don't even *know* him, James.' He only saved my life. Turned my body to flame.

'He's a pretty magnetic guy. Pun that, get it? guy, Guy Reardon.'

Skye waved her hand languidly to acknowledge it. 'So you feel despite his position he might be conniving to usurp my grandfather?'

'Watch it!' James protested. 'I never said that.'

Now James was getting cautious. 'So what did he want?'

'My grandfather wants me back,' explained Skye.

'For how long?'

'God, doesn't that sound appalling! How many years is it, twenty-two? He didn't want me for twenty-two years, now he does.'

'Of course in the bad old days gone by, daughters and granddaughters came in handy,' James pointed out. 'One could marry them off to aspiring young barons and take the edge off their voracious appetites. One might feel guilty beheading one's family.'

'I feel you know a great deal more than you're saying,' Skye charged him.

'So do you.' His twinkling eyes narrowed over her. 'You're a very beautiful girl, Skye, even if you are absurdly modest. You're highly intelligent as well— not good in a woman, if you really stop to think about it. It makes them unhappy, dissatisfied. They fall in love with someone they think is special, then one day they begin to see them with different eyes. Notice a pattern, or a plan.'

'What the devil are you talking about?' Skye demanded fiercely.

'Oh, ducky, how your eyes flash!' he grinned.

'Are you trying to warn me about something, James?'

'Hey, wait a minute, what have I said?'

'I think you're trying to warn me about Guy Reardon.'

'My dear, you're drunk on mineral water. I wouldn't dare set you against a bold mover like Reardon. He would surely be after me.'

'Do you think I should see my grandfather?' Skye asked.

'You'd be mad if you didn't!' James signalled for another drink. 'He *owes* you, girlie.'

'He owes me nothing,' said Skye. 'Nobody owes anybody anything except love.'

James sighed and moved restlessly. 'Love! What a dream!'

'Haven't you ever loved anyone, James?' Skye asked.

'No, dear.' James moved backwards as the waiter set his drink down. 'Infatuated maybe, but it never reached love. I'm very fond of you, and that's superior to infatuation in my opinion. It implies a real caring. Just don't fall under Guy Reardon's influence too easily. Those finely mettled, highly controlled characters are really seething with intrigue. Did you ever look into his eyes? Extraordinary eyes. A visionary idealist with a bit of your dear old grandfather thrown in.'

'Wicked old grandfather, do you mean?'

'People pay no attention to wickedness when it's beautifully presented. Being poor is a crime.'

'That sounded strangely bitter,' Skye smiled at him. '*Were* you poor, James?'

'I left school when I was thirteen.'

She looked at him uncertainly. James was a great kidder.

'I know you find that hard to believe, you with your distinguished father and a couple of diplomas behind you. I had no such advantages. My father was an alcoholic and my mother couldn't get me out of the house fast enough. I made it all on my own.'

'You *did*, James,' Skye pressed his hand. 'But you're so clever, educated, well informed.'

'I was ambitious from the day I was born.' In James's mild eyes there were lights. 'I was so angry I was born to a couple of losers. You don't have to lose if you fight.'

'I suppose that's how Guy Reardon feels,' Skye offered gravely. 'Maybe he feels his father lost but he's not going to.'

'Let's drink to it,' said James. 'Good luck to him, but whatever he's plotting about, he can't have *you*.'

*

Skye was turning the sprinkler on in the garden when Jeremy arrived that evening.

'Hullo,' he said, sounding strained.

'Hullo, Jeremy.'

'Are you on your own?' He looked swiftly towards the house as though he expected Guy Reardon to appear.

'Of course I'm on my own. Excuse me, Jeremy, I have to fix this.'

'I'm sorry.' Jeremy moved backwards, staring rather vacantly at the silvery jets of water. 'Have you decided to sell the house?'

All day she had been fighting back her tears. 'Yes, I'll be selling it, Jeremy.'

'Should fetch a good price,' Jeremy announced solemnly. 'Another great gardener, most probably. It would be sad to see all this go down.'

Skye was silent, feeling she was suffocating with grief. 'Are you coming inside?' she asked.

'All right. I'd like to speak to you.'

No reply from Skye. She was finished with Jeremy and she knew it. Inside the phone rang. 'Let me deal with that,' said Jeremy. He looked tense and aggressive.

'I'll take it, thank you, Jeremy.' Some strange excitement was burning in her. But it was Fiona, her closest friend. They talked for a little while and Skye promised to go over to Fiona's house the following evening.

'I thought that might have been Reardon,' Jeremy said. 'Did you know he's considered the boy wonder of the financial world? Strange for a chap whose father was ruined.'

'Your eyes are flashing messages, Jeremy. What *are* they?'

'If you must know,' he told her, 'Mother and I thought it very odd he should have been here last night.'

'You'd rather I threw him into the street? He did save my life, you know.'

'I appreciate that, Skye,' Jeremy said in a strained voice, 'but he could have stayed in the hospital or gone to a hotel. The sight of him beside you will stay in my mind for a long time.'

'Would you like to stay for tea?' asked Skye.

'You're evading me, aren't you?' Jeremy moved towards her and caught her arm. 'Please, darling, I only want to talk to you. I love you so much I can't feel particularly kindly towards this Reardon.'

'Why on earth not?' Skye's blue-violet eyes were suddenly alight with a strange fire. 'I only met him yesterday for the first time.'

'Yes, and somehow he's turned you inside out!' Jeremy suddenly hit one hand with the other fist. 'Don't think I'm a fool, Skye. Mother surely isn't. She's very experienced, and another woman into the bargain.'

'All right,' Skye looked at him defiantly, 'what does this mean? Are you accusing me of something, as though you have the right?'

'Of course not.' Jeremy suddenly looked apprehensive. 'I'm just so miserable I know I'm not saying this right. I know it's very easy to draw the wrong conclusions, but it seemed to me. . . .'

'And Mother,' Skye cut in maliciously.

'That there was some . . . bond, oh, God, I can't find the adequate word . . . some *attraction*, that's it, between you. You must have patience with me, Skye. We've been together almost a year now and you must know that when I'm a little more established I want to marry you.'

'How established do you want to be?' she asked.

'Jeremy looked at her quickly and smiled. 'Oh, I thought perhaps this time next year. I'm proving myself now. I know I can make it.'

'What's *it*?' Skye asked.

'Everything. You, my job.'

'Let's get married right away.' Skye slumped into a chair and shook her heavy hair back.

'Right away?' Jeremy repeated rather blankly.

'Surely you want that? I know you love me madly. Can't keep your hands off me.'

'My dear Skye,' Jeremy said repressively, 'you've always been able to trust me, as you very well know.'

'You've never wanted to make love to me?'

He reddened. 'Years ago I promised my mother I would never get any girl into trouble.'

'You *what*?' Skye hated herself, but she gave a mad shriek of laughter.

'I can't see what's so excruciatingly funny,' he said stiffly.

'I'm sorry.' Remorse assailed her. 'You're a very decent, honourable person, Jeremy.'

'In fact I've come damn near to kissing you violently.'

'When was this?' Skye decided to press him.

'Oh, lots of times.' He sank down beside her, 'but I'm a little bit frightened of your beautiful wildness.'

'Go on.'

'Don't sound like that,' Jeremy looked at her. 'I expect it will all sort itself out. You're young and your father spoilt you, and of course you have the sort of untamedness that seems to go along with being a redhead.'

'I expect your mother was the first to spot it,' Skye said coldly.

'Mother can't help seeing things. She really understands people.'

'And she thought my father spoilt me?' said Skye in a calm voice.

'Don't you think he did, darling?' Jeremy asked gently. 'Perhaps you were too close to him to recognise it. I meet stacks of people, and they don't have their children in their minds all the time. Your father never thought of anything but you. Everything he did was for you. Why, everything he put into the garden was for you: 'Skye loves magnolias or gardenias or a lot of white in the garden.' I knew I would never have to search for a reason for why he did anything. Why he brought certain books home or records. Why he spent a whole Saturday morning searching for some damned imported cheese because you liked it. . . .'

'A list so long you could live a lifetime before you got through it,' Skye whispered.

'Oh, sweetheart,' Jeremy hugged her, 'I know how careful I have to be. You and your father, two against the world.'

'Yes, I think so.'

Jeremy took her left hand and kissed it. 'Did you mean it about getting married right away?'

'*Would* you?'

He looked helpless. 'It would be better if we held out for another year. An engagement would be perfect.'

'Will you sleep with me?'

There was a pause. 'I want to take care of you, Skye.'

'You don't feel we could be overcome by a powerful passion?'

'We haven't been so far,' he pointed out.

'No. Don't you think that's odd?'

A faintly superior smile crept into Jeremy's good looking face. 'It doesn't just rush for you, darling. You're the master.'

'I guess so. You'd sure get top marks.'

'You wouldn't like it anyway if I rushed you,' Jeremy said triumphantly. 'Gentleness is the thing. All this white-hot burning passion is just another device for the lady novelists. They know most people are mellow, controlled.'

'*I'm* not,' said Skye.

'You're a very complex girl.' Jeremy curled her hair.

'I'm not sure about that. I think I'm just plain passionate.'

'So you are.' He laughed, bent over and kissed her on the mouth.

How long did it take? A few seconds. She opened her mouth deliberately, but Jeremy withdrew. 'My girl!' he said tenderly.

'No,' she said.

'Yes, you are, darling. It's all settled. Now, I'm full of suspense about what you're going to do about your grandfather. It's really *the* most incredible story!'

'Isn't it?' Skye laughed, a laugh full of irony and contempt.

'You're going to see him, of course?'

'You think I should?' She turned to look at him with searching eyes.

'Good grief, yes!' Jeremy looked dumbfounded she should even have to ask the question. 'He may well wish to settle a good deal of money on you. I mean, this is a lovely old house and it will fetch a good price, but there can't be much more. Academics aren't the richest people in the world.'

'In fact we had quite a struggle,' said Skye. 'My father made this place what it is. Mostly with his own two hands.'

'Yes, he was very clever.' Jeremy was genuinely admiring. 'But you don't *have* to struggle any more. It's obviously your grandfather's intention to make it up to you. Why else would he send Reardon? He's *those* Reardons, you know.'

'I must take more interest in Who's Who,' commented Skye. 'In fact until yesterday I'd never heard of the illustrious race of Reardons.'

'Ah well, you and your father did lead such a quiet life until you went to work for Hendersen. Now *he* would know Reardon.'

'Probably.'

'Those sort of people talk the same language. I hope

you don't mind my saying this, but I's always thought Hendersen that least bit common.'

'Sweet of you not to tell him. Did you find Mr Reardon *common* too?'

'Of course not. Reardon's O.K. A bit too much the other way, if you ask me. He's tall enough without holding up his head and looking down his nose. Mother thought him fantastically—dare I say it—*sexy*.'

'Really! What an appalling description, and your mother too!'

'Just a bit of fun,' Jeremy hastened to explain his mother. 'Sometimes she likes a bit of fun.'

Skye swept up as though she just couldn't take any more. 'I'm just going to have something light, Jeremy, cold meat and a salad. Would that do you?'

'Why, yes.' Jeremy moved to the cabinet to fix himself a drink. 'It's just possible, darling, I might be able to land a good job in Sydney. If you've got to go to your grandfather, I won't want to be staying here.'

'But what about your mother?' Skye could scarcely contain herself.

'No problem. I'm sure she would fit very well into Sydney.'

'What do *you* think I should do?' Skye asked her friend Fiona. They were sitting quietly together on the small balcony of Fiona's rented home unit.

'What wouldn't I give for a rich grandfather!' Fiona sighed.

'You'd go?'

'No—I mean I don't know. All I'm saying is it could be rather marvellous to have everything material one wanted. Look at me! There never seems to be a day I'm not overwhelmed by some call on a tight budget. You had your dad. At least you knew how much he loved you, but when my dad remarried I had to go off and live some place else. He never cared much about me and he certainly didn't care about Mum. What a terrible relationship some people have!'

'I think it might have had something to do with getting married before they were mature enough.'

'I think Dad will *always* want someone to push around. This girl he's married, my age exactly, Mum and I feel sorry for her. She doesn't know what she's in for yet.'

'And yet——' Skye's beautiful eyes met her friend's directly, 'it could work out. They seemed very much in tune.'

'Oh, she's right for him,' Fiona said bitterly. 'Poor old Mum never really tried to extend herself from the day they were married. She was *married* and that was it. Our generation have a stronger sense of who we are and who we want to be. Also, the divorce rate being what it is, we *have* to be more independent. I don't know what Mum would have done, only Jon and Pam built that little guest house for her at the bottom of the garden.'

'She's a lovely person, Pam, isn't she?' Skye said earnestly. Not too many young wives would want their mothers-in-law to a degree forced upon them.

'I think Mum loves her more than me,' admitted Fiona. 'I tend to be a bit abrasive.'

'You were only trying to help her, that's all.'

'Damn it all, Mum's only a young woman!' Fiona cried unhappily. 'You'd think she was seventy!'

'Give her time to work it out,' Skye said gently. Fiona really loved her mother a lot, just as she could see the underlying reasons for the breakdown in her parents' marriage.

Fiona shook her head rapidly. 'Poor old Mum! She was taught that all a *real* woman had to do was cook, raise the kids and keep house. Now in her forties desertion for a girl who only wants to get into heavy discussions.'

'Well, your father *is* a politician,' Skye pointed out.

'God, the times I used to say to Mum, won't you even read the newspapers?' sighed Fiona. 'She couldn't seem to comprehend that it was just as important to understand the issues as to keep all those beautifully laundered shirts up to Dad. My problem is, I love him and I could kill him. I love my mother and I could shake her until her teeth rattled! I just can't believe the two of them let it happen.'

'I'm sorry, Fiona,' Skye sighed.

'Ah! You've come over to talk your problems over and I'm crying to you about mine.'

Skye smiled and patted her friend's hand. 'We always were friends.'

'I felt you and your father had the most perfect loving relationship,' Fiona volunteered starkly. 'You could talk to one another about everything!'

'Except my grandfather, of course.'

'Gosh, yes, I never thought of that,' Fiona said flatly. 'It's hard enough taking it in that he's Sir Charles Maitland. I guess your father never spoke about him because he always felt threatened. I mean, some people will do anything for money. And if it's there in the family, they're certainly going to reach out for it as soon as they're able. Your father might have thought you'd desert him for the big time.'

'No.' Skye shook her head.

'No, of course not, knowing you. I think you just might be one of those rare creatures who could turn their backs on a fortune.'

'It hasn't been offered.' Skye directed her face towards the breeze. 'My grandfather has simply come into the period in his life when he wants to put his house in order. I haven't had any contact with him from infancy until the age of twenty-two. The fact is there's no feeling between us except the remembrance of suffering. He remembers and I remember.'

'Couldn't that be a beginning?' Fiona asked

tentatively. 'If people could only talk. If they could only *hear* one another!'

'The idea is to want to hear,' said Skye. 'One can isolate oneself from words. Most of us when we're emotional see only our own point of view. Your father felt your mother had no interest in what he thought of as his real life, that is his public life . . .'

'That's right, she *didn't*!' exclaimed Fiona.

'And your mother felt. . . .'

'Quite rightly. . . .'

'That your father was abandoning her after a lifetime of single-minded devotion.'

'Sad, isn't it?'

'In other words, we tend to stick to our own point of view. My first loyalty is to my father even though I no longer have him. He hated my grandfather, and I'm sure he had good reason.'

'But there's another loyalty isn't there?' Fiona said. 'Family. The strong tie of blood. You said yourself there was a powerful love bond between your grandfather and your own mother.'

'I said there was *supposed* to be, but personally I can't see it.'

'Parents do go off the deep end when their kids race into hasty marriages. Sue's parents, for instance, were pretty voluble when she got herself attached to that Mark Hamilton. They gave them no chance.'

'I think, wisely,' said Skye.

'So do I, but Sue is still full of resentment.'

'Because she feeds them.'

'Exactly my point.'

'You mean you think I'm feeding my resentments?' Skye asked.

Fiona sighed and stood up to make fresh coffee. 'Why don't you give your grandfather a single chance? I've learned something from Mum and Dad. Relationships have to be worked at; they won't keep themselves alive. See your grandfather close to. Make your peace with him if that's what he wants. Maybe it's the time. It couldn't have been while your father was alive. Maybe he needed your total commitment like Dad seems to need Carol's.'

Skye shook her head. 'I don't think I can do it, Fiona. It's hard, a kind of disloyalty to my father, and it troubles me on my own account as well. I don't care that my grandfather is who he is, but some people, my cousins, for instance, could think I'm coming for my share of the money.'

'Really! If he's as rich as they say he is it wouldn't hurt them to *want* a little less,' said Fiona.

'It would be easier for me,' Skye said, 'if he was an ordinary person. As it is, I simply don't think I can do it.'

'All right, love.' Fiona exhaled deeply. 'In a way I hope you say no. I'd miss you dreadfully!'

The day before he was due back in the state capital Guy Reardon telephoned. Skye hated to admit it, but she started shaking just at the sound of his voice.

'Are you ready to come back with me, Skye?' he asked her immediately after he had asked her how she was.

'I'm sorry, I can't.' She took a deep breath and held firm.

'And you're entirely happy about it, are you?' The decisive voice was full of fine shadings.

'Of course I'm not.' Knees shaking, Skye sank down into the high-backed oak chair. 'Don't make me feel worse than I do!'

'*Am* I?' He reigned surprise. 'How are all the bruises?'

'For a while I looked as though someone had mugged me.'

'What did you expect when you go around fighting cars?'

'I'm glad your arm is a lot better,' she stammered.

'I'm sure I can count on it as a permanent little scar.'

'How is it happening that you're making me feel as though I'm being blackmailed?' she chided him.

'Blackmail? What a depressing thought. No, it wasn't as though you owe *me* anything. You're coming with me on your own account. The whole of life is experience. Sometimes we're not happy about what we have to do, but we know we've got to do it all the same. When you started out in life, your grandfather felt the only way he was going to get you was to fight a court battle. No one even bothered to try to work out a solution. Strong passions were involved, and hatred is often a response to unbearable pain. Two men loved your mother. One was her father, the other was a nearly broken young man. The fight pulled them both together and afterwards there were a lot of complex regrets on both sides. I don't think your father could have been entirely happy about cutting you off from your own family. I know the two of you together accomplished a good deal, but your grandfather's world is completely different.'

'And by no means better,' Skye burst out coldly. 'Didn't you tell me my cousin Jo Anne had never worked a day in her life?'

'That was her decision,' he told her mildly. 'There's plenty of room in the Maitland organisation for you to accomplish something if you want to, except that your grandfather is rather hard on the people closest to him—as you might have gathered.'

'You mean *you* had to claw your way up?'

'I'm tough. Of course a lot of people didn't cherish having me around,' Guy told her.

'They didn't trust you?' Skye met her own sparkling eyes.

'You don't quite dare to say they'd be insane if they did.'

'I can't do it, Guy,' she exclaimed all at once. 'Too many mistakes were made in the past.'

'I'm one hundred per cent sure this *isn't* a mistake,' The strong emphasis in his voice rang down the wires. 'It never struck me that you were timid.'

'Don't try the psychology,' she said laconically.

'Aren't you just a little afraid?'

And there was fear at the bottom of it. 'This is getting us nowhere,' she said. 'Besides, I'm trying not to meet you again.'

'Shall I tell you again you lack . . . courage?'

Some note in his voice gave her a violent, electrifying shock. 'I'll come for the weekend, a few days,' she said sharply. 'I've got everything, my whole life, here.'

His tone at once altered, became very businesslike. 'I doubt that we'll be able to take anything earlier than an evening flight. In any case, I'll attend to that. All I want you to do is put a few things in a bag and be ready.'

A few minutes later, with the phone back in its cradle, Skye sat huddled and prey to a thousand tormented thoughts. Guy Reardon had pressured her whether she wanted it or not. She was not really acting on her own judgment. Her own judgment had been to keep to her father's firm stand. What was it now that her grandfather could offer her? Not love, she was sure. How could love flourish out of so much pain? And what frightened her more than anything was the possibility that she might become involved with Guy Reardon again. Whatever their differences and subtle antagonisms, neither of them could now forget how easy it had been to arouse the other's sexuality. She had an intense desire to shut the whole episode out of her mind, but it returned repeatedly, vividly, to haunt her. That was the scary part, the feelings of shame shot through with excitement and the irresistible notion that somehow Guy was playing a game of his own; a game that included her.

CHAPTER FOUR

THERE was a light rain falling when they arrived in Sydney, but Guy spotted the Rolls at once. He greeted the chauffeur, introduced him to Skye, and the two went at once to load the luggage into the cavernous boot.

Moments later and they had moved into the traffic and almost at once Guy and the chauffeur, whose name was Bellamy, started into a mutually profitable conversation that kept up for the entire length of the journey. Bellamy, it seemed, was not only her grandfather's trusted driver, but a valuable aide.

It was only as they stopped before the huge, electronically controlled wrought iron gates that marked the entrance to the Maitland mansion that Guy turned his attention to her again.

'Well, to a new life!'

'You think so?' Her heart was thumping in her chest, but her creamy face was still.

'It's here. As it should be now.'

'How come I'm not happy?' She lowered her voice.

'It will come. A different happiness, Skye. We can't go back.'

'No.' The Rolls was now entering a splendid circular driveway and Skye's violet eyes flickered as she looked towards the house. It was massive in size, brilliantly lit, a magnificent stone mansion of the Tudor lineage with a three-story central section flanked by long wings.

'The daytime view is much better,' Guy told her rather curtly, 'because then you have the harbour.' He took hold of her arm. 'Relax, Skye. Everything will work out.'

The chauffeur was out of the car and Skye trembled as the night air hit her face. Sometimes in her dreams she had come to this place, and even in her dreams she had been sick with nerves.

'Come along, they'll be waiting.' Guy glanced down at her.

'I certainly hope so!' Something in his expression, some faint touch of pity, aroused Skye's spirit. She shook her hair back and looked upwards towards the open archway through which light poured. A great basket-shaped chandelier was appended from the ceiling, glittering in the grand manner, and in spite of herself, she felt an ache of pleasure at the beauty of her surroundings. So this was how the wealthy lived! She was to find out twenty-two years later.

In the beautiful panelled entrance hall several people were awaiting her. 'Skye, my dear child!' An arrow-slim, very elegant woman in her late forties hurried towards her, the long dark red skirt of her dress swirling from the thighs. 'Welcome!'

Skye had to steel herself to accept a kiss on both cheeks in the French manner, for her sensitive antennae told her the woman was taking great care to be gracious. 'Thank you,' her blue-violet gaze was wide and searching. 'You're Aunt Felicity?'

A tiny, humorous little grimace. 'Please, dear, just Felicity! Now come and meet the family. Grandfather is resting upstairs. I had to *make* him. Someone has to remind him to be careful about himself.' She caught Skye's hand and drew her towards the assembled group, throwing a brilliant smile over her shoulder for Guy's benefit.

All Skye's instincts were in top gear now. Her uncle Justin, with a distinguished, long thin face, greeted her with a mixture of gladness and a painful sadness. 'I hope, my dear, we'll be able to spend a lot of time together,' he said.

There was Jo Anne, very dark, very pretty, smiling

her mother's brilliant, unrevealing smile. 'I hope we'll
be friends, Skye. I must say we couldn't be more
unalike!' Her eyes rested on Skye's flaming hair as
though she marvelled at the colour.

Warren. He drew her towards him urgently and
pressed a far from cousinly kiss high on her
cheekbone. 'I've been wondering and wondering what
you'd be like.'

A patrician, rather sombre-faced girl stood close
beside him, her resemblance to Guy Reardon enough
to mark them as family but not striking. The
introduction wasn't necessary, but Warren made it.
'And this is Adrienne, Guy's sister, of course, and
soon to be my wife.'

'How are you, Skye?' asked Adrienne after what
seemed like an overly long time. 'You're far more
beautiful than anyone imagined.'

'She's Deborah,' her uncle said, and his strong voice
trembled. 'The image of Deborah.'

'Of course she is!' Felicity's face was suffused with
some answering emotion. 'Poor Grandfather!'

'Shall I upset him?' asked Skye in some concern.

'He's had a mild heart attack,' Felicity exclaimed,
and her husband settled her with a look.

'He's longing to see you, Skye,' he reassured her.
'Obviously he's excited as we all are, but you mustn't
think there's any cause for worry. My father is an
extraordinary man.'

'Why don't I take Skye up to meet Grandfather?' Jo
Anne asked. She was now standing beside Guy, almost
leaning against his shoulder, her two arms locked
around one of his. She wore a slim-fitting green dress,
and though she wasn't a genuine beauty she looked
extremely attractive and sumptuously sure of herself.

'I'd like that,' said Skye.

'No need.'

A voice stopped them and they all turned to look at
the tall and upright elderly man who had reached the

first landing of the divided stairway. '*Skye*!' she heard him say, yet she was rooted to the ground.

'Go to him, for God's sake!' Guy Reardon was beside her, his voice barely above a murmur, yet it shocked her out of her unnatural calm.

She moved towards the stairs, too strained to feel any sort of embarrassment, and then it hit her how desperately fearful her supposed tyrant of a grandfather was of *her*. His thick hair that had once been as red as her own was pure silver and the unmasked blue eyes begged her almost hopelessly to be forgiving and gentle.

'Grandfather,' she said, her face exquisite with warmth and sorrow.

Guy Reardon, watching tautly, was proud of her, and yet not everyone there so silently applauded her. Sir Charles started rather blindly down the stairs, but Skye went to him, her mind spurning the old griefs because she couldn't hold out against that handsome, worn face. Startlingly, she even *looked* like him.

'My dearest, dearest child, can you ever forgive me?'

The question was too much for her to answer, but Skye went into his arms, astonished at the flood of healing warmth. To be reconciled in an instant after all the years of bleakness and rejection? Yet the shakiness of his long sight moved her profoundly. 'You're the most beautiful sigh I've ever seen!' The words weren't planned or considered but the result of the deepest, heartfelt emotion.

Jealousy struck home, flashing from Felicity to her daughter in a chain reaction. Their menfolk apparently were calmly accepting it as though their own joy in reunion was immeasurable. Adrienne Reardon, too, saw the peculiar radiance in her fiancé's face and because she was highly intelligent understood it was not put there by any feeling of family but because of how his new cousin looked and moved and spoke. He was enchanted by her. Adrienne could discern the fascination in his face and she, too, felt a violent thrust of jealousy. Had Guy brought this girl all this way for Warren to be irresistibly attracted to her? Adrienne directed a shuddering glance towards her brother, only to have him, very levelly, return her look. Guy never missed anything. Not *anything*. She had first realised that when she was a young girl and they were the best of friends. Now there was an unease between them and the knowledge that Guy had never been in favour of her engagement to Warren.

They all moved into the great drawing room with its splendid marble mantel, vaulted ceiling and luxurious furnishings, with Skye and her grandfather seated on one of the sofas and the rest of them arranged around them. Because of the immensity of the room only the area where they sat was lit by dazzling shafts of light; the far end of the room with its high, arched leaded windows was almost in deep shadow.

'I should leave you,' Guy announced suddenly.

'But, my boy!' Sir Charles looked up with real regret in his face.

'I promised I'd call in on my mother.'

'Oh, please stay to dinner, Guy!' Jo Anne stood up in a quick movement and flowed to him.

'Really, I can't,' he apologised gracefully, but it was apparent he wasn't going to be persuaded. 'Besides, this homecoming is for—family.'

'And we certainly owe a great deal to you.' Sir Charles turned to face him, the pink colour of pleasure tingeing his cheeks. 'How can I thank you?'

'Oh, I'll think of something.' Guy's handsome mouth twitched.

'I've no doubt you will.' His agitation abating, Sir Charles was just beginning to exhibit the sharpness he was famous for. 'I'll be in my office tomorrow morning about ten o'clock. I'll be glad to see you.'

'Thank you, sir.' Strangely the smile didn't quite

reach those shimmering grey eyes. 'Goodnight, Skye. I'm perfectly sure I'm leaving you happy.' His eyes swept over her, moved to the upright, imposing figure of the old man.

All if a sudden, rather desperately, she wanted to go with him. 'I'll see you again?'

'Of course.'

'I'll walk with you to the car,' Jo Anne offered a little gratingly. 'Bellamy is driving you, isn't he?'

'Yes.'

'Guy?' It was Sir Charles again.

'Sir?' Guy was the only cool one there.

'I want to know what's going on with Mainstay.'

'I *told* you, Father,' Justin Maitland said quietly.

'I'm sorry, Justin,' Sir Charles's blue eyes flickered. 'I'd like a report from Guy here.'

Guy glanced at both men, his dark face enigmatic, and said calmly, 'I'll bring it to you in the morning.' It was a neutralising tone of voice and it seemed to break an awkward silence.

'Well now, if you must rush off,' Felicity came towards him and clutched at his arm with almost the profuse eagerness of her daughter, 'you'll be free next Saturday, won't you? You and Antonia, of course. Grandfather wants to give a little party for Skye. We must introduce her to our friends.'

Skye couldn't stop herself then. 'Really, Aunt Felicity . . . *Felicity* . . . I don't see myself in a party mood. I've just lost my father!'

Sir Charles nodded and looked stricken. 'Of course, of course, my dear.'

'And we truly understand,' Felicity seemed to smile. 'Perhaps I didn't put that properly, my dear. *Not* a party, merely an opportunity for you to be introduced to society. It's expected, you know, and it will be good for you.'

'I really don't know how long I'll be staying,' Skye faltered, but only for a second.

'You're not staying?' Jo Anne looked intrigued and pleased.

Sir Charles took a deep breath. 'Is there anything urgent you have to get back to, little Skye?' Unlike his other granddaughter he looked bewildered and stunned.

'I'm sorry, Grandfather,' Skye felt his hand shake under her own. 'I haven't made up my mind.'

'But you've decided on at least a month to six weeks?' Guy Reardon's voice was filled with a smooth persuasiveness.

She sighed in answer, wavering even as she looked into his diamond-bright eyes. 'Of course.'

'I'm glad. *So* glad.' Sir Charles, to many so distant and remote, let his feelings show. 'You don't have to do anything you don't want to do.'

'But you would like me to meet people?'

'Just that. Meet them—perhaps at a small dinner. No parties—not yet.'

'Fine!' Felicity's expression became brisk and approving as Skye seemed to accept what she was required to do. 'Antonia will be free, won't she?' she asked Guy.

'I'm not too clear on my mother's plans,' Guy Reardon glanced down at her, dangerously attractive and curiously remote.

'I'll ring her.' Felicity too seemed perplexed by what she couldn't see in his eyes.

'Goodnight, sir.' He glanced over Felicity's stylishly coiffured head. 'Skye.'

'Goodnight, my boy.' Sir Charles nodded, but Skye stood up suddenly and went across to him, holding out her hand.

'Thank you.' Her voice was just a little bit fearful. 'I can't forget how . . . good you've been to me.'

'I wish you'd tell us,' Jo Anne said playfully, staring from one to the other.

'Me too.' Warren apparently shared his sister's

mischievous streak, a warm, rather challenging look kindling in his dark eyes. 'Did he find the time to make you fall in love with him?'

'Oh, for God's sake, Warren!' his father said, in a short, disgusted way.

'All the girls fall in love with Guy,' Warren confirmed, unrepentant.

'That will do, Warren,' said Sir Charles bluntly. 'If you can't see your conversation is distressing, you'll have to be told.'

'I'm sorry.' It was a little pathetic the way Warren retreated to a small boy. 'I was only having a bit of fun.'

'But, darling, this is a very solemn moment,' Felicity told him, smiling away her own resentments. 'It's a pity you have to rush off, Guy, but at least it gives Jo Anne an opportunity to see you to the car. I think she's been pining ever since you went away.'

Skye knew she was meant to see exactly what the position was. Guy was for Jo Anne. Poised and glossy, Felicity would break anyone in two who tried to get between Guy Reardon and her daughter.

'Please come and sit beside me again, Skye,' Sir Charles called, and Skye, who had no desire to stay where she was, immediately obeyed. She had come to make peace with her grandfather, not complicate her life with jealousies and intrigues. And it was jealousy she saw, in at least three women's eyes. As for the future—she had promised Guy Reardon a month, six weeks. She had a feeling it might seem to be a very long time.

Much later that night, as Skye was moving about the exquisitely decorated room that had been allotted to her, her cousin Jo Anne tapped on the door, then opened it before Skye could even articulate a reply.

'Hi there!' she said, in a friendly fashion, her nearly black eyes just that bit surprised at the brilliant elegance of Skye's robe. 'May I come in?'

'Of course.' Really Skye could think of no other reply than that. Secretly she had been hoping to find a good friend in her cousin, maybe even love and affection in time, but now she didn't believe for a moment that Jo Anne would ever be her friend. It was essentially instinct and the suspicion that Jo Anne found her very dull and earnest. She remembered the expression of Jo Anne's face at dinner when she was discussing the increasingly important role public relations people were playing in business. It was almost a copy of Jeremy's mother's muzzy boredom when Skye advanced an opinion on anything but fashion or how beautifully Mrs Phillips managed the food and flowers. Clearly both women thought they were meant to be jewels and not concern themselves with the power struggle or the development of their brains.

'Happy with your room?' Jo Anne asked.

'It's dazzling.' Skye cast an appreciative eye around the soft opulence of the room. 'I've never been in anything one half so grand.'

'You should see mine!' Jo Anne turned to head so she see herself in the mirror. 'I like your robe.'

Skye dipped her head. 'It was a present from my father.'

'I'm sorry, Skye.' Jo Anne sank down on the edge of the Georgian fourposter bed and draped her arms around a gleaming column. 'I've heard very little about your father.'

'He was everything in the world to me.'

'A pretty girl like you?' Jo Anne looked sceptical.

'Surely no one can be closer than a parent?'

'Hey now, you look upset!' Jo Anne's dark eyes went wide. 'All I meant was you must have lots of boy-friends?'

'I don't have lots and I don't want lots,' Skye shook her head and tried to smile.

'That's just talk.' Jo Anne suddenly threw herself back on the bed. 'There's nothing a woman likes better than plenty of admirers. Even Mamma has her fans, though she never makes Daddy too mad.'

'Your mother is a very stylish woman.'

'She works at it,' Jo Anne said casually. 'She's far more disciplined than I am. Occasionally I break away from my diet, but Mamma isn't given to accepting failure.'

'I suppose a certain amount of it is part of life,' Skye observed.

'My dear, not in *this* house.' Jo Anne stretched her slender, olive-skinned arms. 'That's why Warren infuriates us all.'

'Warren?' As Jo Anne had the bed, Skye dropped into an armchair.

'Sometimes I think the only way to stop him is clamp his jaws. It's little enough Grandfather asks of him, but to be frank he's not Maitland material.'

'And what *is* Maitland material?' Skye asked.

'Oh, you know, someone who can bear the burdens of power. All Warren can do is luxuriate in its trappings.'

'You mean he's not a business man,' said Skye.

'Of course not. Neither is Daddy, for that matter, though he's got plenty of brains. I wish I knew exactly what it is that goes into making men like Grandfather and Guy—and don't worry, they may look like good friends to you, but they're locked in some power struggle.'

'But surely Guy works for your ... *our* grandfather?'

Jo Anne laughed. 'As Daddy says, Guy works for himself. Himself and what's left of the Reardon family. A classic rise and fall. Guy's father committed suicide, you know.'

'I didn't know.' Skye *had* heard it, but she didn't care to hear it again. 'It was confirmed, was it?'

'No, but it was so obvious. The idea of losing all that his family had worked for was too much for him.

The Maitland corporation is always expanding and Grandfather had been interested in the Reardon projects for some time. Reardons managed to hold on to a lot of their shares and I guess Grandfather is holding on to Guy to ease his conscience, or better yet, keep an eye on him. Daddy said it's impossible to keep Guy in his proper place. We're all beginning to wonder if he won't rest until he's sitting in Grandfather's chair.'

'I see.' The silence lengthened.

'Of course he's devastatingly attractive,' Jo Anne moaned. 'Don't you think so?'

Skye knew better than to show enthusiastic agreement. 'He's certainly very striking,' she said quietly.

Jo Anne sat up, smiling at her. 'You must have been surprised Grandfather sent him instead of one of the family?'

'After twenty-two years, Jo Anne,' Skye said calmly, 'I'd given the *family* up.'

Jo Anne's rather doll-like eyes flew open even wider. 'But there was no alternative, Skye. Surely you understood. Your father wanted no part of any of us. You must know deep down it was *his* fault.'

'To be pushed too far!'

'Heavens, let's forget about it.' Jo Anne was checked by the sudden blaze in Skye's violet eyes. 'It had nothing to do with us really. We were just kids, and kids must do what the adults say. Sometimes I think men always treat women as kids. Do what you're told and I'll provide everything for you to make you happy.'

'I'm surprised that you've said it,' remarked Skye. 'Aren't you happy, Jo Anne?'

'Of course.' Jo Anne stretched voluptuously, 'or I will be as soon as I've landed my man.'

'Guy Reardon, for instance?'

'He's so perfect,' Jo Anne sighed. 'Passionate and

tender and really formidable, as a man should be. Sometimes I'm sure he wants me and other times he's just as far away as the moon. Of course Antonia doesn't like me,' she added rather fiercely, 'and Adrienne is such a cold bitch. God knows what Warren sees in her.'

'And Antonia is Guy's mother?'

Jo Anne nodded mutely. 'She never lets us forget this was *her* house. She just sits and looks around. We never come to words or blows, but we all know.'

Skye blinked several times. From the beginning she had sensed some deep, unknown force in Guy Reardon. Now to hear that this beautiful place had been his family home. . . .

'Do you mean this house belonged to the Reardons?' she begged for confirmation, her young face stricken.

'No big mystery!' Jo Anne shrugged. 'There was no way they could have held on to it, and this is without doubt one of the most desirable residences in the whole country. The original Reardon estate covered about five acres, but Guy's grandfather sold off a few acres to some of his pals. Lady Daniels is on one side of us and the Bryants on the other—you know, the architect for the Inman building. They have a fabulous place too, not as grand as here, but very beautiful and more contemporary. You'll be meeting them. Robb does a lot of work for Grandfather. He has extensive property interests.'

'They must have very much minded losing it,' Skye said.

'They haven't bought another house since,' Jo Anne sighed. 'I guess it must be terrible when your whole world is swept away. Guy's father, Julian, was very much the gentleman. Grandfather says "gentlemen" always make a mess of things, but really he was so handsome, and so *nice*. Mamma believes he was too nice. Had he been more ruthless, of course, like Grandfather, it mightn't have happened, but

Grandfather always clamps down on what he wants. He went after Reardons and he got it.'

'And what precisely did Reardons *do*?' Skye asked.

'Really, you're asking?' Jo Anne exclaimed.

'I don't know much about big business.' Skye's violet eyes travelled over the petite figure of her cousin.

'Well ... let's see. They operated an electronics plant in four States. That kept them terribly busy. Then there was Rankins, heavy equipment makers, that belonged to them. They took over Youngmans when it wasn't doing so well. Youngmans made hospital equipment. Of course there were little ventures on the side, but you couldn't really be interested in them?'

'I can't see how they lost it,' said Skye.

'Of course, Skye,' Jo Anne said dryly, 'you don't know Grandfather.'

'And what does Grandfather own?'

Jo Anne threw herself back on the bed and closed her eyes. 'Three times as much as that again. We just keep growing and growing. If you want to know so much, have a little talk with Daddy. He'll recite it all to you like a litany.'

'I will,' Skye answered seriously. 'I must say I'm astonished Guy came to work for Grandfather.'

'*I'm* not!' said Jo Anne with a little crow of triumph. 'It's better to have men like Guy right under your eyes. At least that's what Grandfather says. We've all shut our minds on what happened, you know.'

'Except that the past has a terrible reluctance to die,' said Skye quietly.

It only took Felicity a few days to broach the subject of Skye's clothes. 'You'll need more, dear,' she announced, giving Skye's simple, relaxed dress a kind smile.

'I think I have enough to hold out,' Skye returned politely, anxious to avoid spending money.

'Nonsense!' Felicity couldn't restrain the exclamation. 'I insist on taking you shopping. I'm quite sure you didn't bring along a dinner dress?'

Skye nearly said, 'I've worn it.'

'If you're imagining you'll have to spend a lot of money, don't worry,' Felicity went on, at ten o'clock in the morning done up to the nines and with not a hair out of place. 'Jo-Jo and I simply love shopping, and it all goes on the account.'

'Well, that's splendid for you, but I can't take advantage of it, Felicity, I'm sorry.'

'Ugh! Don't tell me you're going to be difficult about spending a little money? How ridiculous. Besides, Grandfather *wants* you outfitted with a complete wardrobe. He'll be very much offended if you refuse his kind offer.'

'I'll see him myself, Felicity.' Skye moved quickly. 'I don't think he's left yet.'

'Oh, Skye!' Felicity called, but Skye only turned briefly and gave Felicity a wave. She was reluctant to have any kind of gift showered on her. Only last night her grandfather had handed her the most exquisite jade carving and when she expressed her delight, smoothing the flowing robe of the female figure, most probably a high-ranking court lady, her grandfather told her casually that it was Sung dynasty and he considered she should have it. She, too, had that same grace and elegance. Of course she declined, she hoped with grace, and her grandfather had not pressed her.

When she tapped on the study door he called a gruff: 'Come!' but the severity in his face disappeared as soon as he saw it was Skye. 'It would be splendid for me if I could stay at home today,' he said. 'The really important thing is for you and me to get to know each other.'

'Why don't you, then?' she smiled.

'Ah, dearest, I can't.' His voice sounded harassed. 'How I long to get rid of. . . .' he muttered something to himself.

'Looking for something?' Skye moved helpfully around the desk.

'Yes. A file marked Private and Confidential.'

'I always say there's nothing like a good, tidy desk,' observed Skye.

'I agree.'

'Would this be it?'

Sir Charles shot a glance at the extended file, grasped her around the shoulders and kissed her cheek. 'You must be the only one in the household who can find something!'

'You look a little tired, Grandfather,' she said.

'Didn't sleep much.' He visibly straightened his back. 'Tell you the truth I was thinking about you. How different this house is with you in it. Surely you can't go off and leave me?'

'I hope we're not going to talk about leaving. I've just arrived.'

'You're like your mother even to the way you laugh.' The still intensely blue eyes reflected an underlying misery. 'We shall have to talk one of these days, Skye. You'll have to let me tell you the way it was.'

'Are you quite sure it will help?' she asked gently.

'It will help *me*.' His expression eased. 'Do you know that once my hair was as red as your own?'

'Guy told me people used to think you were a lion on the loose.'

'Goodness, I haven't heard that one for years! Fancy Guy telling you.' Sir Charles kept one arm around her and picked up his briefcase. 'I wish you would think about staying with us for ever, Skye,' he said. 'I don't really think I could bear losing you now.'

'Now, now, don't get gloomy.' With her free hand

she opened the door. 'One of these days I'd like to come into the office and look around.'

'I'll arrange it,' said Sir Charles. 'We'll have lunch in the boardroom. We might even ask a few people. Now what about this little dinner party Felicity wants to give? You mustn't think you have to do anything you don't want to.'

'That's what I wanted to talk to you about,' Skye plucked up her courage. 'I really don't need a lot of new clothes, Grandfather.'

He hesitated, looked down at her and smiled. 'You must be the only woman who doesn't!'

'I think I have all that's necessary.'

'I see.' He was looking down at her with a grave expression. 'I suppose Felicity suggested shopping?'

'I thought. . . .'

'Yes?'

'You mightn't particularly like the sort of clothes I wear?'

'My dear, I don't actually see them. I'm too busy looking at *you*. Surely you must understand why. But as far as that goes, why not go along with Felicity and give her pleasure. You're a beautiful girl and you're young and all that. Women love shopping, don't they, and it would give us all the greatest pleasure to see you in some new finery. You never have to worry about money again—I mean that, Skye, and you mustn't tell me you don't want anything I have to offer. I've gone through such hell it's important now that you let me make up for the lost years. I know you can get along without a new wardrobe, but you mustn't stop us from trying to give you pleasure. Shopping is Felicity's way. Isn't it nice she wants to take you?'

'Yes, of course.' Skye met her grandfather's eyes a little helplessly. 'I don't think I could get used to having a lot of money, Grandfather.'

He just laughed and patted her on the shoulder. 'You know there's more to life than money, worldly success. Money won't go to your head. It's never gone to mine either. Sometimes I think it's better to start at the bottom and work up or, alternatively lose everything and have to fight back.'

'Like Guy?'

'Like Guy,' Sir Charles seconded quite comfortably. 'His secret dream is to topple me. He doesn't quite know yet how he's going to do it, but I get a funny kind of pleasure just watching him. He ought to have been my grandson, but the truth is my grandson might just as well be racing cars. I can't think why no one has inherited my business head or even my nerve. It's just like watching children. Then there's Guy. . . .'

Skye walked with her grandfather to see him off. At the base of the stone stairway the Rolls was parked with Bellamy sitting inside, lost in the pages of one of the morning newspapers. 'Did your father ever speak about me?' Sir Charles asked suddenly.

'Not often, Grandfather,' said Skye, treading warily over dangerous ground.

'I remind myself that he hated me,' the old man mused.

'He saw the world through the past.'

'But he loved *you*,' said her grandfather with respect and a certain amount of envy. 'And he reared you well. If only both of us hadn't fallen victim to a terrible paranoia. God help us, we both loved your mother so much.'

CHAPTER FIVE

THE evening of what Skye thought of as 'Felicity's little dinner party', she dressed with great care, excited and sobered in turn. Two weeks now and she had only spoken to Guy on the telephone, and then only by chance, because he had wanted to speak to Jo Anne. It had given Skye a tremendous, much-needed jolt and reminded her scaldingly of the night she had been ready to give herself to a man she didn't even know and who didn't even care. The humiliation was appalling, and Skye decided as she answered him with reserved politeness that she would never put herself or him in such an outrageous position again. He might have *seemed* to want her badly, but to understand it better, both of them had been very much shaken by the events of that extraordinary day. In her fragile state she had craved physical comfort and he had simply reacted to her heightened femininity. Ah well!

Skye sat down at her dressing table, trembling with nerves. Tonight her hair, newly styled, had a flamboyant life of its own. Naturally full of body, cutting into the curl had set it free all down its length, so it flared up and away from her face in bright wings and flowed just a little past her shoulders. Such a mane made her face look especially small and because she had used much more eye make-up than usual, the size and colour of her eyes seemed doubly intensified. In fact, she considered she looked 'all eyes' until she balanced the effect with a deeper colour on her mouth, a sumptuous burnished rose. Normally she did very little to accentuate its fullness, in truth, a little fearful of a certain luscious quality. Tonight, however, she had to make up to the dress, a long gold lace that was at once demure and very sophisticated. It was a superb colour with her skin and hair, and Felicity had insisted that it was necessary if she was going to merge into their world at all. She had even gone so far as to lend Skye a pair of Edwardian, pendant-shaped gold earrings to go with it, and they threw little lights against her cheeks. Jo Anne, she knew, would look stunning in a raspberry couture creation, and Felicity told them casually she would be wearing an ultra-smart black.

Both Maitland women took dressing incredibly seriously. Skye would have described it as a career. She would always remember the day they went shopping together. It was a bit like a Royal procession, with boutique owners pressing their hands together to try to stop themselves from clapping. Both women had gone along with all the flattery that flowed around them, while Skye turned her eyes away from the price tags in shock. They couldn't possibly be worth that much, and she knew it. Felicity and Jo Anne had been remarkably unimpressed. Of course they had the means, but it seemed immense self-indulgence to go after more when one already had enough. Still, there was no denying they both looked as sleek and elegant as a pair of cherished greyhounds. They really only saw themselves in terms of beauty and desirability, but Skye knew she couldn't possibly fit into the good life without a good deal of guilt. Obviously whether her grandfather settled a little money on her or not, she would have to work. Her personality was anything but passive or stationary. She needed to function to at least something like her full potential. Her father as an educator had insisted that a woman's brain was every bit as good or as bad as a man's. Indeed, between his students it had been difficult to choose. Her father had expected her to graduate with a first-class diploma, and because of his attitude she had gone on to achieve their goal. Not all her friends had received the same encouragement and support—her girl friends, that was. Skye was often struck by the difference in what was expected of boys and girls. Sometimes she wanted desperately to change it.

Half an hour passed and Skye encountered Warren in the long gallery. 'Skye—my God, you look gorgeous! A walking tiger-lily!'

'I'd like to be a bit taller.' She smiled at him, feeling a rush of affection. Like his mother and sister, Warren was smoothly, darkly good-looking, but whereas the women's self-confidence took the breath away, it was plain Warren knew himself to be something of a disappointment.

'I can't imagine why you would want to be. You're perfect!' His brown eyes touched on her glowing hair, the apricot-tinted cream face, and continued down along her throat, the delicate richness of her dress, to her gold-sandalled feet. 'It just goes to show you can give even a glorious natural product a helping hand. I don't think I knew your eyes were quite that big, or your mouth would send a man mad.'

For a moment Skye was embarrassed by his enthusiasm. 'It must be the make-up,' she said lightly.

'Whatever it is, it's fabulous!' Warren still had no idea he was staring at her as if mesmerised or that he had picked up one of her hands. 'Before you arrived, we thought there might be a few problems, but you're a real asset.'

'What problems?' Skye felt a frisson of upset.

'Forget it.' Warren laughed gratefully. 'What amazes me is that it took so long to get you into our lives.'

'Surely you could have come to see me?' she challenged.

'The plain fact it, would you believe it, it never even occurred to me. If you've never seen your cousin, you don't feel you have one.'

'Maybe,' she looked back at him a little gravely, 'but I've always dreamed about family.'

'Well, you've got one now.' He pulled her to him a little shyly, vaguely thinking to hug her, but there was some electricity about her that he suddenly realised had disturbing overtones. She wasn't his cousin any more. He wondered if he had ever thought of her as his cousin. She was an exceedingly beautiful girl he wanted to move much closer into his arms.

'Warren?' Skye's own thoughts were muddled. Warren was still holding her, looking down at her almost hungrily. Now he leaned forward and dropped a kiss on her nose.

At that moment someone coughed ostentatiously and followed it up with a dry greeting, 'Hi, you two! Getting better acquainted?'

Warren flushed and dropped his hands swiftly. 'Just come here and have a look at Skye.'

'Show me, Skye.' Jo Anne breezed forward, bright, assessing eyes checking every point of Skye's appearance.

'Sure.' Smiling a little wryly, Skye obliged. Sometimes Jo Anne looked and acted so much like her mother it was incredible.

'And *you* didn't want to get that dress!' The approval in Jo Anne's eyes gave way to a faint hardness.

'I wanted it all right,' Skye looked down at herself. 'I just couldn't steel myself to pay the price.'

'You'll have to get it sorted out just who you are,' Jo Anne told her bluntly. 'You may have been used to a limited budget, but you can't use that any longer as an excuse.'

'Oh yes, I will! I'm not paying these prices every day.'

'How ungracious of you,' Jo Anne said jeeringly. 'While you're here, you're part of the Maitland team. That means it's important for you to look good.'

'Don't get hysterical!' For once Warren overrode her. 'Skye would look good in an old sugar bag, which is a damn sight more than I could say for you.'

'Yes, I know. You've seen me in a sugar bag, I suppose?' Jo Anne's expression made it clear she cared nothing for her brother's opinion. 'Anyway, Skye, you look terrific.'

'Thank you.' Skye felt a little aghast. 'So do you.'

'Of course.' Jo Anne smoothed her hand down her body with a thoroughly feline gesture. 'The Maitland women are supposed to be an asset to Grandfather.'

'You know, at parties, not board meetings,' Warren said with bitter sweetness. 'Is sitting around all day being an asset, dear sister?'

'What difference does it make sitting around here or there?' Jo Anne countered. 'Grandfather is proud of me—that's what sticks in your throat.'

Sickened and unhappy, Skye looked down at her hands so she didn't see the flash of hatred in Warren's dark eyes. 'Goddammit, you're a bitch, Jo Anne!' he shouted. 'You always were!'

'Oh, please!' Skye risked the intervention. 'Aren't we going to have a pleasant evening?'

'Of course we are.' Warren made an effort to get hold of himself. 'You must have gathered by now, Skye, that I'm a profound disappointment to my family.'

'I don't know how I could conclude that,' Skye said quickly, upset by the tremble in his voice.

'Why do you think Grandfather approves of his engagement to dear Adrienne?' Jo Anne questioned, almost viciously. 'The Reardons are clever. Adrienne was so busy collecting degrees we never thought she'd have time for marriage. As far as I know they haven't topped Guy in brilliance. Grandfather reasons that a marriage might bring some much needed vigour back into the family. And now, if you'll excuse me——' Jo Anne bowed rather contemp-

tuously and swept along the gallery, a glowing figure
in her beautiful dress.

'I'm sorry, Skye,' Warren said. 'That must have
been upsetting for you.' He gave a low, a bitter laugh.
'Jo Anne and I have fought since we were children.
She's always been impatient of me, and she really
dislikes Adrienne.'

'Don't feel badly, Warren,' Skye said quietly. 'I
think I understand Jo Anne and you.'

'What made her so angry anyway?' Warren asked
moodily. 'Didn't she like you to look as well as you
do?'

'Of course she did.' With dismay Skye heard the
lack of conviction in her voice.

'I happen to know Jo Anne better than you do,' said
Warren. 'You have no idea how she played up when
she heard Guy was being sent after you.'

'What did she possibly think would happen?' Skye
asked a little sternly.

'Hell, I don't know,' Warren was still quivering
with rage. 'That he'd fall for you, I suppose. Jo Anne
has a great affection for Guy. As far as I'm concerned
she should forget it, but Mamma and Jo Anne are
really determined types. To hear Mamma talk you
would think they were practically engaged!' His brown
eyes held a wounded expression. 'It's a funny thing to
know all your life you're a disappointment.'

'Don't talk like that, Warren. Don't even *think* it.'

'Ask anyone,' Warren shrugged. 'Might I remind
you, our grandfather is a man of great influence and
power. He didn't inherit a business empire, like Julian
Reardon, to carry on. He built one—from nothing. He
came here as a poor little immigrant, now he's one of
the richest, most successful men in the country. It's a
hard act to follow. Dare I even say Dad has trouble
walking in his shadow.'

Skye looked up into his eyes, seeing the suffering.
'Being a rich and successful business man isn't

everything in life, Warren,' she told him. 'There are a good many other things to be. Maybe better things. It doesn't really matter what we are so long as we can bring some contribution to the world and feel pretty happy with our own identity. You sound to me as if you've been engulfed by Grandfather, his aura, his world. If you don't have his abilities, it doesn't make you less of a human being. You should think more positively about yourself. I know you'd be good at the things you enjoy. Isn't it possible to accept then that you're not such a great business man? My father was considered to be a fine scholar, but I attended to all the household management, did the budgeting.'

'I bet your father treated you as an equal.'

'Well, we're all roughly equal,' Skye smiled.

'It's no joke, Skye,' Warren said bleakly. 'How can I accept what I'm not, when no one will let me? I can't say, "Right, I'm off and that's the end of it!" '

'Why not?'

'Why *not*?' He looked down at her incredulously. 'My darling girl, you might have lots of energy and purpose, even, you have Grandfather in your make-up, but *I* fear to strike out on my own. I fear to lose my inheritance. I've grown up rich. Do you know what that means? It means I'm still a helpless kid clinging to Grandfather. He's the initiator, the one with the brains and the drive. God, none of *us* could make a fortune! He's central to everything. We'd all be desperate if he suddenly abandoned us. For years Mamma was terrified he might do something crazy and marry some woman young enough to have a child. Mamma is so greedy, she wants the lot. What if Grandfather changed his will and left most of it to you? We wouldn't be able to continue. Without Grandfather in control, by the time Dad got his mouth open Guy would hold the chair. I'm not being funny either,' Warren assured her. 'There's some manic ambition in Guy. He's supposedly on our side, but my mind keeps slipping back to the old days before the Reardon crash. So far as I'm concerned, Grandfather is old and the writing is already on the wall. In which case, my services will be terminated.'

'Surely you're the beneficiary of a trust?'

Oh, yes, of course. I'm not madly rich, though, Skye. In fact I'm little better than well provided for.'

'Then why are you so unhappy? It's a pretty sad old world, after all. A lot of people are having a very nasty time of it.'

'I know I'm lucky,' Warren said hopelessly.

'And you're being too hard on yourself. You haven't failed anyone, Warren. You're just expecting too much of yourself. Very, very few people can be described as brilliant. You should decide that you're perfectly normal. Like the rest of us.'

'Except I'm surrounded by people who aren't normal,' Warren said in a low voice. 'I thought when Guy came along and grabbed so much of Grandfather's attention I'd be as hostile as hell, and Dad does resent him bitterly, but Guy's kind. Can you beat that? *Kind*! I didn't believe a person like that *could* be kind. I've never been game to ask Grandfather anything, but if I ever ask Dad, he gets so irritated, I have a terror of asking him anything at all. In desperation once, I had to ask Guy when I was in some difficulties with a contract, and he actually took the time to run through it all and explain it. He sees everything at once, like Grandfather, but he doesn't rattle the life out of you talking too fast. He's an odd fellow, Guy. With you and not with you, if you know what I mean. I know he doesn't want me to marry his sister.'

'Why not?' Skye had thought the same thing herself.

'I'm still trying to figure that out,' Warren said with some perplexity. 'I know she loves me. God knows why, but she does.'

'You're unfair to yourself, Warren,' said Skye, her flaming head tipped to one side.

'And you're very nice to your new cousin.' Warren leaned slighty towards her, absorbed by the play of light in her hair, the reds and golds and the ambers.

Once more Skye felt a little awkward, so she turned and moved a few steps along the gallery, lined with fine paintings in heavy gilt frames. 'I suppose we should be going downstairs,' she said lightly.

'I guess so.' Warren followed her, giving the decided impression that he was happier where he was.

Skye took pity on him, waited, and gently took his arm. 'You're going to have to help me this evening. I'm not used to these dinners.'

Abruptly Warren pressed her arm to his side and laughed. 'Not yet!'

At last Guy and his mother, Antonia, arrived, and Skye prayed her extraordinary agitation would not betray her and glitter out of her eyes. Guy was turning away from Felicity with a slight bow, then Sir Charles was performing the introductions, drawing Skye forward so Antonia Reardon could look at her.

'How beautiful you are, my dear.' Antonia Reardon's melancholy eyes had flashed at the first sight of her. 'Were such a thing possible, even more beautiful than your mother.'

'Thank you.' Skye looked deeply into the older woman's eyes, gauging her sincerity, but there was nothing there but gravity and a slightly startled friendliness. 'I should love you to tell me about my mother some time. You must have known her.'

'Enough to have the sight of you disturb me.' Antonia Reardon kept hold of Skye's hand. 'I would be glad to have you visit me any time you like. Guy would bring you, I'm sure.'

'I'd like that.' Skye smiled back at the etheral figure.

Antonia Reardon looked almost unbearably frail, unbearably lonely. In her mid-fifties, her wonderful, shining eyes were all that was left of a delicate beauty that had all but burned away. She was wearing a dress of black chiffon, relieved by a triple string of the most exquisite pearls, and her heavy dark hair was coiled ornamentally at the back of her head. Her daughter Adrienne was very much like her, with the same faintly morbid expression, only not so tiny. Beside her son, so tall and frankly stunning, she looked as stylized as some exotic doll.

'You look well, little one,' Guy said gently, taking her hand.

'I was about to say the same of you.' She forced herself to meet his brilliant eyes.

'Shall we make a day right now?' his mother suggested.

'Why not?' he agreed gently, not before he had brought the back of Skye's hand to his mouth and barely kissed it.

'Let me see,' Antonia Reardon fingered her pearls. 'Guy usually has dinner with me of a Wednesday. Would that do?'

'*This* Wednesday?' Shivers were still running the length of Skye's arm.

'Would you rather another time?'

'No, Wednesday would be lovely,' Skye gave a small laugh. 'I'll look forward to it.'

'So will I.' Antonia looked and sounded faintly surprised.

Twenty, in all, sat down to dinner. The long dining table shone with a polished richness, its dark lustre aglow with antique silver and china, the sparkle of crystal and the lovely low floral arrangement of glossy green leaves and white carnations that ran almost the length of the table. A steady stream of delicious things flowed from the kitchen by way of black-uniformed, white lace-trimmed female attendants, and Skye sat through it all as though she had spent a lifetime being waited on.

Felicity, she noticed, often smiled approvingly when this or that was set down, but never once did she murmur 'thank you'. The staff were there to do their job, for which they were very well paid. Skye even had the peculiar feeling she had stepped into some film set, so glamorous was the whole scene.

The men wore black tie as a matter of course and the women guests were very handsomely turned out. Indeed Lady Daniels, from next door, wore diamonds on her splendid bosom and her tinted hair was an incredible platinum halo around a rather violently made up face. She contributed a lot of talk, verging on scandal, to the conversation, which no one appeared to take seriously, and even Antonia Reardon relaxed her desperate tension and gave an amused chuckle.

'I don't believe that, Maggie,' she said.

'It's true, darling. I only heard it this afternoon and saved it up for tonight.'

'You're outrageous, Maggie!' someone else said.

Lady Daniels put a hand over her heart, then theatrically clutched her own ample breast. 'You know, this girl here is making me feel quite shivery! It seems as though twenty years have rolled back and Deborah is sitting among us, looking around with those same violet eyes.' She smiled at Skye and her own rather piercing scrutiny gentled. 'Welcome home.' She lifted her wine glass, and Sir Charles said: 'Maggie!' and lifted his too. 'To my granddaughter, Skye.'

They all toasted her and Skye stifled a sigh, wanting so badly to respond wholeheartedly but held back by her own grief.

'It really is wonderful how everything has come right again.' Lady Daniels told them all, not missing the swift, silent communication that passed between

Felicity and her daughter. 'It must be wonderful for you, Jo Anne, to have your cousin.'

'I've been thanking God ever since,' Jo Anne returned the challenge squarely.

'Perhaps Guy would be better. They say he found her?'

Not surprisingly Felicity changed the subject and Lady Daniels began to tell her neighbour another one of her slightly ribald but definitely upper-class jokes. Dirk Bryant, the architect, seized the opportunity to ask Skye to visit them and his wife, Anne, a charming and intelligent woman, began to ask Skye about her interests.

Eventually it came out that Skye was working for James Hendersen.

'And who is this Hendersen feller?' Sir Charles, looking flushed and happy, asked.

'A public relations consultant,' Guy told him. 'He has affiliates here.'

'I told you, Grandfather,' Skye said.

'*Did* you, darling?' Sir Charles frowned. 'Perhaps I had more important things on my mind.'

'You handle most things, don't you, Skye?' Guy Reardon looked across the table.

'Not political liaison. Conventions, marketing and public relations programmes, tourist promotion publications, research, writing. . . . I started with James soon after I gained my diploma in Business Communications.'

'You *what*?' Lady Daniels looked both impressed and astonished. 'Do enchanting young females go in for Business Communications?'

'This one does.' Skye gave a little laugh. 'It's very interesting really.'

'I should find it a terrible bore,' Jo Anne drawled.

'I don't think you would if you tried it,' Skye answered without rancour. 'A lot of girls took the course. Finding jobs had rather more to do with it than usual. Many graduates can't find work. My father wanted me to become a teacher, but I didn't really want to do that at all. I guess I'm a doer. James calls me a born business woman.'

'No such thing!' Sir Charles laughed indulgently and patted her hand. 'Women have no head for business at all. They haven't the vision or the aggressiveness. They can't gamble with high stakes or cope with setbacks. Supportive is what they are—what they're supposed to be. Excellent at that sort of thing . . . routine.'

The put-down always did this to her, generated body heat, but Skye managed to speak mildly. 'Women haven't been *allowed* to be good at business, Grandfather, which is a vastly different thing.'

Two or three of the guests moved back in their chairs, benumbed. It was obvious Sir Charles didn't quite like this, but Jo Anne with her passion for mischief decided to stir the pot. 'What's this?' she asked gaily. 'Are you contradicting Grandfather?'

Skye didn't hesitate, her beautiful eyes full of zeal. 'What I'm saying is women can do big jobs just as well as the men. They *are* doing big jobs. Just how many women in business do you suppose know their boss is a bit of a fool? Or their male colleagues who get promoted regardless while they have to accept that they've come to a dead end. Women aren't lesser beings there to do the donkey work, they have every bit as much to contribute.'

'Hear, hear!' Guy put his hands together, but didn't smile. 'So you, for one, haven't been brainwashed.'

'And what is that supposed to mean?' Jo Anne looked at him uncertainly.

'On the other hand,' Sir Charles cut in smoothly, 'women don't really *want* to get anywhere. That's their problem.'

Guy seemed to frown at her, but Skye continued.

'Their problem is,' she said spiritedly, 'it's been made almost impossible for them in a male-dominated world. A world, incidentally, that's in a wretched mess. Maybe men could do with little less aggression or have their aggression balanced by a woman's more sensitive perceptions. I would like us to work together, but it's extremely difficult.'

'Might I say you're rather aggressive yourself,' Jo Anne said playfully. 'Maybe it's a result of being a career woman.'

'Do you think a woman shouldn't speak directly?' Skye challenged her.

'They've always called *me* blunt,' Lady Daniels tried to catch Skye's gaze. She was far more spirited than her mother, Lady Daniels was suddenly realising, and she sensed that Jo Anne was all out to make trouble.

'Finally,' said Skye, and laughed to make a joke of it, 'some of women's troubles lie in themselves. They ridicule their own sex.'

'Surely Jean McIntyre would make a good sales manager?' Guy said suddenly.

'Good lord, no.' Justin Maitland looked shocked.

'Why not?' Guy seemed to be looking not at, but right through the older man. 'She's far more competent than Mason.'

'But—yes, well, she can't deal with the men.'

'That won't hold up, Justin. Times have changed. Perhaps too slowly for young crusaders like Skye. Jean can handle the men. Me included. I'm going to recommend her promotion at the next board meeting.'

'Goodness, surely we're not going to talk business,' Felicity said a little feebly.

'You're being rather provocative, aren't you, Guy?' Sir Charles said, frowning. 'I know the McIntyre women is surprisingly good at her job, but women don't make for smooth management.'

'Precisely because they're not given a go.'

'*Please*, my dear.' Sir Charles really wasn't interested in Skye's unsolicited opinion.

'I think it would be a damned good idea if the Maitland Corporation upheld women's rights,' Guy said crisply. 'You'd find they'd flock to us. We're only tapping half the brain power. Adrienne sitting so quietly over there was recently knocked back for a big job for which she's highly qualified.'

'Oh, but——'

'No buts about it, sir.' Guy responded rather icily. 'She lost out not on qualifications, but prejudice. We all know the man who got the job, Bill Morrison. A good man, but Adrienne was best qualified. Not everyone on the board rejected her, but one man's influence carried the day.'

'I hope you're not suggesting *I* had anything to do with it,' said Justin Maitland.

'Did you?' Adrienne asked unexpectedly.

'My dear, you're soon to be my daughter-in-law.' Justin Maitland's long, thin face looked pained.

'That's not answering the question.' Guy Reardon's penetrating gaze moved from his sister back to his colleague.

'Surely I don't need to be asked.'

'I ran into Butler yesterday,' said Guy. 'We had a bit of a talk.'

'I'm quite sure Butler talks too much,' Sir Charles said. 'Now suppose we continue this discussion in the library while the ladies catch up on all the gossip?'

Adrienne stayed behind to have a few quick words with her brother and Skye walked along with Antonia Reardon.

'What did she expect?' Antonia sighed.

Skye gave the older woman a sharp look. 'You mean Uncle Justin voted against her?'

'Of course he did, my dear. You know there's a great deal of tension between our families.'

'But it's so jumbled,' said Skye. 'Guy works for

Grandfather. Adrienne is going to marry Warren.'

'Much against my wishes.' Antonia was allowing her eyes to roam all over the house. 'We used to have a Russell there,' she pointed to a space on the wall. 'You know, the painter—John Peter Russell, our first Impressionist.'

'I know.' Most of Skye's interests were artistic. 'He did that wonderful portrait of Van Gogh.'

'Yes.' Antonia's gaze was infinitely sad. 'There's little substance to Warren and a great deal to Adrienne. They *can't* be happy. Naturally Guy is disturbed about it too.'

'Can one actually control feeling?' queried Skye. 'Caring in the wrong place?'

'I'm absolutely certain she doesn't love him,' said Antonia. 'She has never really bothered with anyone, you know. Her father's tragic accident shattered her life. She was a different girl before that. We were *all* different. Guy was never so. . . .' She sought for a word and couldn't find it.

'I can understand how dreadful it was,' Skye said feelingly.

'No goodbyes, nothing. He just went out.'

'Please come and sit down, Mrs Reardon,' Skye said gently, and took the older woman's arm. 'Being in this house must make you feel too much.'

'But then, you see, he didn't have to buy it,' Antonia explained.

'My grandfather?'

'The auction fetched a whole lot more than anyone expected. Because your grandfather wanted it that badly.'

'Do you hate him, Mrs Reardon?' Skye asked gently.

'Of course not. I'm beyond hate.' She sounded quite sure. 'There's only one other person I've ever seen contradict your grandfather, and that's Guy.' Antonia turned to the girl beside her and began to smile. 'That showed spirit all right! Your grandfather hasn't begun to realise it yet, but you've got lots of it. The point is, however, how is he going to take it?'

'He can't reject me, if that's what you mean, Mrs Reardon,' Skye said. 'My character has been formed— my father did that. I've come here to demonstrate to my grandfather that despite everything I do have some love for him.'

'And *do* you?' Antonia moved her delicate shoulders.

'It's hard not to with one's own flesh and blood. I look like Grandfather, haven't you noticed?'

'As a matter of fact, I have,' Antonia's voice was amused. 'He's still a handsome man, but years ago he could only be described as devastating. But hard— always hard. You're a different person. You have your mother's sweetness and compassion and a whole lot of your father. I only met him once, so I never could understand how your grandfather was bent on destroying him.'

'You mean the court case?' said Skye, flushing.

'I mean there was no real reason for your grandfather's violent opposition to the marriage. Your father, from all accounts, was a fine young man.'

Tears started to form in Skye's eyes and Antonia shook her head in dismay. 'I'm sorry, my dear—sorry! One can't bring up the past. All we can do with it is bury it and let it haunt us in our sleep.'

When the men emerged from the library it was to find the women sitting in the drawing room in little groups, and Lady Daniels immediately jumped up to entertain them on the piano. Once, before she had married her late, industrialist husband, she had had a career in musical comedy, and it soon became apparent she could turn an excellent voice to something funny, much in the way of the comedienne Anna Russell.

'She could have made her fortune, Maggie,' Guy said when he came up to Skye. 'You look gloriously beautiful tonight. But there is one thing you lack—a quiet tongue.'

'I'm glad to find you can get your mouth open as well!'

'Sometimes I think we're living in the Dark Ages.' He put out his hand to her. 'Come outside on the terrace.'

'Why? It's pitch dark out there.'

'I can turn on a half a dozen lights.' He gripped her hand and she came gracefully to her feet.

'You'll need to explain yourself to Jo Anne,' she pointed out composedly, conscious of her cousin's sharp gaze.

'I wasn't aware I had to explain myself to anybody.' His voice had a warning undertone.

'Aren't you lucky! What a wonderful thing it is to be a man!'

'Well, don't think I expect you to show the proper female subservience,' he told her.

'Did Uncle Justin answer your question?' she asked as they moved through the open french doors out on to the perfumed cool of the terrace.

'Your uncle finds answering any of my questions very inconvenient.'

'Then why do you work with him?' Skye spoke softly, but as always, to the point.

'I serve my family,' he said.

'Ah, an extremely sensitive point.'

'Speaking of sensitive points,' he looked at her, 'you appear to have dazzled Warren. He's been looking wild-eyed at you all night.'

'Warren has?' She took a step backwards so that leaves of a flowering vine caressed her spine.

'Doesn't he realise you're here on the basis of *family*?' A kind of lightning flashed out of his eyes.

'I'm sure you're mistaken.'

'Such a damn fool thing, to feel romantic about the relations.'

'That's not funny!' She looked around as though expecting a jealous fiancée was about to rush her. 'I know Warren likes me.'

'My dear,' Guy drawled insolently. 'he's so taken with you one would think my sister bores him to tears.'

'Perhaps you should arrange my return ticket home.'

'Not yet.' He regarded her for a little time, but still there was a muffled droning in her ears. 'It could be a kindness if you got some kind of cousinly act together.'

'Are you suggesting I'm trying to fascinate Warren?' Skye asked laconically.

'Not at all,' he said soothingly. 'In a way it could even detach Adrienne from his side.'

'Don't use *me* in your machinations,' she whispered.

'What did you say?' He moved suddenly and grasped her arms, the long falls of golden light making magic of her dress and hair.

'Don't take me for a fool!'

'Of course I don't.'

'I won't become involved in any of your plans,' she said firmly.

'You're already involved.' His grip tightened.

She looked at him. Out here in the golden gloom it was dangerous, his magnetism for her carried to excess.

'*Please*, Guy!' It was a plea she wasn't even sure she uttered.

'Please what?'

'You know very well what I mean.'

'That something happens when I touch you?'

'That's right. I bruise easily.'

'Do I seem to be hurting you? I'm only holding you very lightly.'

'And I don't want it,' she said tautly. 'You're such a devious-minded devil!'

'Who's creating waves around here?' he mocked her. 'I don't think Sir Charles had ever been contradicted in his whole public life.'

She laughed, and it sounded a little strange. 'Someone told me tonight you often obey the strong urge to do so.'

'It's not very good for either of us, is it?' His thumbs were moving rather caressingly over her skin.

'*I'll* never fit in here, Guy. I don't feel or act the same say as the rest of them. I was hoping Jo Anne and I could be good friends, but underneath it all, she's hostile and I don't blame her. Grandfather isn't terribly tactful in his mode of expression. I've been forced upon the rest of the family.'

'Have they let you know this?' he asked, somewhat crisply.

'It won't take Jo Anne long to make no bones about it, and when that happens I'm taking off. I mean, who needs them? I have my home to go to. I hope I have still have my job.'

'I'm sure you have,' he responded a little sarcastically. 'I told you Hendersen is very taken with you—not just with your undoubted capacities, which incidentally could be put to good use *here*, but those positively *female* things about you like a beautiful body and an intense little face. A pity to mention them, but nevertheless they're there. That's the whole other thing about women on the job. One can't altogether deal with biology. We might want to focus on a beautiful woman as the boss if she could only get past the fascinated attention.'

'I can't see anyone really fascinating *you*,' she commented tartly. 'And I assure you, in a crisis James thinks I'm one of the boys.'

'But you're not that.' Before she could protest he dropped the merest kiss on her mouth. 'Not from where *I* am.'

High heels clattered on the cool marble flooring,

then Jo Anne came into sight, her words faintly hectoring.

'Darling, come on! There's a party going on inside.'

'Yes, I know. It's *my* party,' Skye said dryly.

'Then why don't you get back to it?' Jo Anne was staring from one to the other as though she could actually see the pulsing air.

'The thing is, Jo Anne, we're quite settled here for the moment,' Guy gave her a charming, half rueful smile. 'I must do what I can to make Skye feel at home.'

'Grandfather doesn't like it,' said Jo Anne. 'He really can't bear to have Skye out of his sight.' A flash of uncontrollable jealousy sounded in her voice.

'Look at it this way, Jo Anne,' Skye said. 'It may be that Grandfather is taking special notice of me now, but I'm sure, given another few weeks, things will revert to normal. I'm not staying here, you know.'

'If it's up to Grandfather you will.'

'But it's *not* up to Grandfather,' said Skye, her voice full of conciliation. 'I know it would be best for us all if I went home. Besides, my perverse nature revolts against the good life. I want to get back to work as soon as I can.'

'How unbelievable!' Jo Anne exclaimed, a note of derisiveness in her voice. 'I can't really believe in career-orientated women, you know. I thought they might be women too plain to get a husband.'

'Curiously enough, plain women seem to stay married longer,' Guy offered as though bent on working out relationships. 'Now Mrs Mahoney, that's an Irish lady who "does" for me, as she puts it, has been happily married for the past thirty years and I think she would classify herself as downright homely. Her husband definitely isn't. As you say, it's mad-sad.'

'I suppose we'd better go in,' said Skye, turning her head.

'Yes. Grandfather will be annoyed, and you don't want that.' Jo Anne went to Guy and took his arm. 'Now, I'm going to hold you to that promise to take me out sailing on Sunday. The weather should be perfect and we haven't been out for such a long time.'

'Will you come too, Skye?' He lifted an eyebrow and looked towards Skye, her blazing head caught in a soft downlight.

'Are you out of your mind?' she said calmly. 'I can't swim.'

Guy's expression clearly showed he didn't believe her, but Jo Anne laughed explosively. 'Warren told me you were like a fish in the water. I suppose you just got sunburnt together.'

'No, I don't like sunbaking much either.' This wasn't the case either, but it was safer, far safer not to cross into Jo Anne's territory.

Now she smiled sweetly. 'Oh, well, you haven't lived on the harbour like we have.'

'Or had a good time on Queensland's wonderful beaches.' Languidly Guy looked down on her. 'Jokes aside, little one, there'll be an opportunity again.'

CHAPTER SIX

'GRANDFATHER wants you in his study,' Jo Anne told her the next morning as Skye was reading a most curious letter from Jeremy.

'Oh, all right.' Skye broke off with a start. She would have to wade through this later.

'You seem to get a lot of mail,' Jo Anne pressed her. 'You seem immoderately interested in that.'

'I'm positively enthralled.' Jeremy had written a week ago to tell her he was eager to take up a position in Sydney, now as she read his latest letter painstakingly it was apparent he had somehow manoeuvred his way in to the Maitland organisation. That was the sort of thing Jeremy would do—aided and abetted no doubt by his mother. Maitland's had a big legal department and she knew Jeremy was excellent at Company Law. 'A friend of mine,' she explained a little awkwardly. 'He's shaken me a bit. It says here——' she found the place, 'he's just recently had an interview with a Mr Hugh McKenzie. . . .'

'Hughie,' Jo Anne broke in grimly. '*Our* Hughie?'

'After which he's been invited to join the Maitland legal department.'

'Oh, that stinks!' Jo Anne said scornfully. 'Did you suggest him for the job?'

Skye folded the letter and stood up. 'Why in God's name would I do that? I don't want Jeremy here.' All at once the absurdity of it struck her and she began to laugh. 'What a frightful mess!'

'Perhaps you should decide if you really want these admirers before they start shifting house,' Jo Anne commented.

'Maybe I should send him a telegram,' Skye countered. 'Oh, goodness.'

Jo Anne saw her twist the letter into a sort of bow. 'Why don't you stick with him,' she said shortly. 'Guy—don't think I didn't notice you last night—is far beyond your reach.'

'You're right, he's not easy to figure out.' Skye was perturbed by Jeremy's letter and Jo Anne's obvious hostility, but she made an effort to communicate. 'Why are you so angry with me, Jo Anne? You've been angry since I first came here.'

'I haven't.' Jo Anne shifted her dark gaze to the gloriously blue sweep of the Harbour.

'You can't know how much I wanted us to be friends.'

'Yes, well, it's obvious we can't!' Jo Anne had the grace to look a little embarrassed. 'How do you think it feels for the rest of us? We're just stick people. Grandfather has always had very little to say to me, but he's always noticed I'm here. Since you've arrived, or since your father died, you're the first priority on Grandfather's mind. Personally I think he's become a little unhinged. He's spending more and more time at home, and he just longs for your company. I'd say, in someone like Grandfather, it's pretty pathetic.'

'Then you don't understand him at all,' Skye pointed out quietly. 'I don't think he's really seeing *me* at all. It's my mother he has back at last. Can't you allow him to find a little peace? *I've* had to. I didn't come here easily, you know, Jo Anne. In a way I thought, still think for that matter, it's a disloyalty to my father. He never wanted our paths to cross, but he always allowed me to make my own decisions. I did decide.'

'Yes, dear,' Jo Anne agreed with a bitter, twisted smile.

'What does that mean? Surely you have the courage to tell me.'

'Oh come off it, Skye!' Jo Anne jeered. 'To put it unpleasantly, you're here for your cut. And you're entitled to it—don't think we all don't know that. What we're worried about now is that Grandfather might do something entirely mad.'

'You mean settle on me something more than my fair share?'

'No doubt you've thought it yourself.' Jo Anne sat down quickly as though her knees were weak. 'I hate myself for being jealous of you, Skye, but I am.'

'No need—truly, no need.' Skye put out her hand and brushed it lightly over her cousin's glossy hair, 'I'm not interested in Grandfather's money.'

'I might even believe you,' Jo Anne admitted. 'But *you'll* have nothing to do with it. I think Grandfather has already spoken to Daddy about changing his will. You were left something I know, but Daddy thinks it's going to be a whole lot more.'

'Then I shall do something positively philanthropic with it,' said Skye. 'I'd like that. I have no grandiose ideas for myself. I'd like a nice big home where my children can grow and perhaps not having to worry about money, but I don't need a mansion filled with antiques and too much security. I never want to be in the position where I have to worry about my children. They can set off for school by themselves and not be taken in a Rolls.'

'*And* picked up.' Jo Anne smiled. 'You're an odd creature, aren't you, Skye?'

'I don't think so. It's you, my cousin, who's had the extraordinary life. Why didn't you go on to university?'

'Secretly I wanted to,' Jo Anne confessed. 'But I made no effort at school and I simply didn't qualify for a place.'

'You could have tried again. Everything is a lot easier when you get into the right mental state.'

'I don't think I could have borne it,' said Jo Anne.

'Anyway, there was no need to work. We're supposed to work for money, and we have plenty of that.'

'I think, if we're lucky and we have the opportunities, work is what they say, a salvation. I would be very miserable sitting around all day.'

'It's okay.' Jo Anne yawned. 'You must remember I'm used to it, and Mamma particularly likes to have my company.'

'Of course she does,' Skye said in a low voice. 'My father and I used to do lots of things together.'

There was a pause and Jo Anne looked up with quite a different expression on her face. 'You know, Skye,' she said in a concerned, sympathetic voice, 'I wish I could have known him. I wish Grandfather had never made the mistake of behaving so severely, then we could have grown up together. I can see you might have taught me to think properly.'

Sky was touched and heartened. 'I'd have liked that very much,' she said a little emotionally. 'But as far as I'm concerned we can start off together right now. I want a cousin, and I think you need one too.'

Sir Charles was stretching out his long legs when Skye finally arrived in the study. 'You wanted to see me, Grandfather?' Because she was a naturally demonstrative person she moved towards him and hugged shoulders in an embrace.

'To tell you the truth,' Sir Charles caught hold of her arm and held her to him. 'I couldn't face not seeing you every day. Not now. Not ever again.'

'Well, I'm just another granddaughter,' she smiled.

'A very precious one.'

'Jo Anne is under the mistaken impression you've forgotten about her,' Skye said quietly, interlocking her fingers with the old man's. 'It's easy for feelings to be hurt when you love someone.'

'Has she been complaining?' Sir Charles asked a shade uneasily.

'Of course not, but you *are* making much of me, and I thought we might defuse a potential little situation.'

'Can I help it if I love you better?' Sir Charles looked up at her with an ironic smile. 'Neither of my other grandchildren have ever held my hand or treated me with that lovely ... casualness you do. If I ask Warren a question he goes pale, and nobody would take any notice of Jo Anne's chatter. She doesn't seem to have a brain in her head. And she thinks she can attract *Guy*! She'll have to think again.'

'I wonder, Grandfather, if you're not a little hard on them,' Skye said. 'Probably they're both a little daunted by you. You see, you communicate a definite image. You're very clever. You don't suffer fools easily, and although Warren and Jo Anne are far from foolish, they don't appear at their best when you suddenly speak to them.'

'Then why don't *you* jump out of your skin?' Sir Charles appeared to be astounded. 'Why do *you* find it so easy to relax with me, or find it no great effort to make intelligent conversation? Or, for that matter, take me to task at dinner.'

'I'm sorry,' Skye said quickly. 'Did I seem to do that?'

'Yes.'

'I bet that was a first,' she said lightly, then laughed.

'I thought you were going to start that chaining yourself to the table.' Sir Charles looked up at her, sitting so gracefully on the side of his armchair.

'I should have been coaxing you,' Skye smiled. 'Do you really think, Grandfather, that women aren't as intelligent as men?'

'Yes, I do.'

'No hope for you, then.' She bent down and kissed his cheek. 'You see, you're as much a victim of a myth as a lot of my own sex.'

'Dearest, I don't feel in the mood for an argument,' Sir Charles said, but still he smiled.

'I'm not going to argue with you,' she said. 'I'm going to show you. Give me a job.'

'No!' This very definitely.

'All right—then I won't stay. You can't expect me to sit around like a lounge lizard.'

'Like your cousin, you mean?'

Skye was immediately sorry she had chosen that phrase. 'No, I don't mean like my cousin. I don't wish to be unkind at my cousin's expense—it was merely a phrase. But I do want a job, Grandfather, and if you won't give me one, I'm going home.'

'This is your home.' Behind his heavily framed glasses, his eyes flashed.

'Well, you see then, I have two. And I have a very beautiful garden that only a neighbour is looking after at the moment. Decisions have to be made.'

'Indeed they have!' Sir Charles said, taking control. 'It must be obvious to you that I don't intend to let you go. When you left here as an infant I made the worst decision of my life—probably the worst decision a grandfather could ever make. I believe now I helped kill your father. He loved Deborah no less than I did, but instead of offering one another mutual support, we turned into mortal enemies. I've bitterly regretted the things I did and said, and I believe your father had cause for regret too. He said many things to me that were harsh and cruel. We each blamed the other for Deborah's death—but of course neither of us was to blame. I still don't understand how she slipped so easily out of life. Women are such frail creatures. Childbirth—my God! I don't think I could handle seeing you or Jo Anne carrying a baby.'

'That was *one* tragedy, Grandfather, twenty-two years ago. You have to believe that it won't happen again. Millions of babies are born safely. Women will always want them whatever the risk and these days the risks are fewer than they've ever been.'

'That's true.' Sir Charles sighed deeply, suddenly

looking old and tired. 'I'm not as tough as I used to be, Skye. I have to have you near me now until I die.'

'Well, you needn't sound as though it's going to be within the week.' She gripped him again with young strength. 'Now, what about that job? If I'm not good, you can always fire me.'

'What the devil do you want a job *for*?' he challenged her. 'I mean, despite what you say, women are happiest at home.'

'Not all women, and none of them if they haven't enough to do.'

'But you've only just arrived!' Sir Charles cried. 'I think this is absolutely idiotic, my granddaughter working for me! Good God, I'm working so my granddaughters don't *have* to.'

'But this one wants to, don't you see?' Skye caught at her grandfather's firm chin and turned it up to her. 'Get this straight—I'm a chip off the old block.'

She thought her grandfather would smile, but disastrously the remote, the powerful, the formidable Sir Charles Maitland gave a shuddering, dry sob. 'Work if you must,' he said jerkily. 'The only dread I have is to lose you.'

Guy didn't look at all surprised when Skye mentioned it to him the following Wednesday night. He had called for her at the house, now he was driving her to his mother's penthouse apartment for dinner.

'Grandfather was a little hostile at first, but he gave in at the finish,' she told him.

'You must have been very persuasive.' He glanced at her briefly, his eyes sliding over the delicately determined profile.

'I said I would go home,' Skye admitted.

'How dare you say that!'

'I meant it,' she assured him.

'Believe me, Sir Charles knows it. You're very like him in some ways.'

'That's what I told him,' Skye smiled. 'I'm a chip off the old block.'

'You mean you're a transformed edition.'

'That sounded rather acid,' she commented.

'Would you say so?'

'Don't try that enigmatic style with me, Guy Reardon. I know you're really seething underneath.'

'If that's right,' he said dryly, 'why are you sitting there so relaxed? I might feel half crazed enough to stop this car and make love to you.'

'You can if you really want,' she shrugged.

'No, little one, I won't call your bluff.' He laughed gently in the back of his throat. 'So what else do you want to do?'

'Something in my own field, of course. I can't help knowing there's a few objections about that new plant you're putting up at Smithfield. What about if I present it all nicely? Set the locals' minds at rest. Explain what we're going to do and how we're going to do it. People feel a lot better about things if they're properly informed. I've already read the environmental study.'

'Have you now? Where did you get it?'

'Off Grandfather's desk.'

'Shouldn't you have waited?' suggested Guy.

'No.'

'All right, then, show us a layout of what you think we should do. Of course, apart from the environmental study you'll have to make yourself totally informed. You'll have to see the site, speak to a lot of people.'

'You've only got to get me a car.'

'Tomorrow, if you like.'

She smiled. 'When you look at me like that, I'm convinced I can do it.'

'Hendersen referred to you as a very smart cookie.'

'How vulgar! Which reminds me,' she said on an impulse. 'Jeremy—you remember Jeremy?'

'Indeed I do.'

'He's found himself a job in the legal department.'

'*Our* legal department?'

'No, don't!' Skye held up her hand. 'I have a feeling you're about to tell me off.'

'What the hell!' His black, winged brows came together in a frown. 'Did you tell him to apply?'

'I did not. Before you get really worked up, I did give Jeremy to understand our friendship had gone as far as it could go.'

'I'm not surprised, he seemed so genteel.'

'Should a man be ridiculed because he doesn't force a woman into bed?' Skye asked drily.

'Who's talking about force, violet eyes?'

'You're not going to let me forget it, are you?' she said bitterly.

'Why should I? *I* can't.'

You're a magician, she thought. You don't even have to touch me to make some parts of me fly and others melt. Cool reasoning was her best protection, or more accurately, bodyguard. 'What we have to understand,' she said clinically, 'is that we were responding to the terrible tensions of that day. Also, both of us had had a pretty savage shake-up—you more than I.'

'You definitely majored in psychology,' Guy said drily.

'You *know* you understand.'

'Is that what scares you, Skye?'

They were turning into the underground parking lot before Skye's heart began to slow. 'We'll be right on time,' she said in the lift.

'My mother is looking forward to seeing you again.' Guy was leaning back against the wall, staring down at her.

'She's very lonely, isn't she?' Skye said.

'Very.' His eyes were so silver they were transparent.

'You should get married,' she said seriously. 'Both

of you, you and Adrienne, should get married and give her grandchildren.'

'You've said that before.'

'She wants a little grandchild to love. A woman can have lots of things to love, but she always loves children best.'

'Well, my wife had better love me,' Guy said firmly.

'After you, I meant. You're going to need a lot of a woman's time.'

'Tell me.' On the opposite wall the light for the penthouse gleamed.

'We really haven't got time.'

'Suppose you tell me afterwards when we go home in the car?'

'Skye!' Inside the penthouse, Antonia came forward, smiling. Tonight, in comparison to the evening she had come to Felicity's dinner party, she seemed totally relaxed. 'Darling,' she reached out to her son with one and clasped Skye with the other, 'this is really delightful.'

'How lovely it is here!' Skye said sincerely. The apartment block was in a very fashionable and historic part of Sydney, but the usual box-like interiors had been offset by architectural detail and dramatic walls of glass that afforded the fortunate occupants the most spectacular views of modern Sydney and its magnificent harbour.

'It was difficult indeed to pick out which things I most wanted to keep,' Antonia said. 'As you can see, this whole apartment would just about fit into our old drawing room, so it was a bit of a problem paring down. Guy has his things, of course, and Adrienne knew definitely what she wanted, but we had to auction the rest.'

'To be frank, Huntingdon would be much too much for me,' Skye told her. 'It's a masterpiece, I know, but the size defeats me.'

'You'll get used to it,' said Antonia, 'just as I had to

get used to a massive reduction in space. I used to start off in a great hurry to get absolutely nowhere. No stairway, no long gallery. I suppose it was time-consuming, at that.'

While Guy fixed them all a pre-dinner drink Antonia showed Skye the rest of the apartment. It might have seemed humble to the Reardons, but to Skye it was dazzling in its assemblage of beautiful contemporary and antique furniture, the superb, museum quality paintings and objects and the lovely soft colour schemes.

'Of course, I had the help of an interior designer,' Antonia explained, 'an old friend, actually. He has worked for me before both at Huntingdon and the beach house. We're always in perfect accord.'

'And he must delight in being able to use such wonderful things from your collections.'

'I suppose so,' Antonia sighed. 'I hadn't thought about that.'

I'll bet *he* has, Skye thought. It was precisely this acceptance of wealth and all it could provide that vaguely upset Skye. Antonia, even Felicity and Jo Anne seemed very far removed from real life. And what was the result? Not one of them was happy. It was better, Skye thought in reaction, to make one's own way. She was even grateful she had been reared in an ordinary middle-class background. At least she couldn't break her heart living in an environment most people would consider rich and splendid. At least Adrienne had made the effort to break out of her golden cage. She had a very impressive background in computer science, an area of technology her father and brother had directed her towards. Guy, she already knew, had a master's degree in Electronic Engineering. In addition, because of the high demands that it was anticipated would be placed upon him he had other appropriate diplomas in Management and Marketing. Julian Reardon had obviously seen to it that his children would be able to stand on their own two feet if ever his business empire collapsed or was sabotaged. The inference seemed to be that the Reardon take-over was one of her grandfather's notoriously greedy impulses. At the very least Antonia believed it, and despite his position of importance in the Maitland organisation, Guy left one wondering if his view of the situation was any different. The Maitland men were certainly of the opinion that Guy was only waiting for Sir Charles's eventual demise to fix them all for good. Maybe there was a ferocious obsession behind those shimmering, silver-grey eyes. Skye almost felt like a helpless martyr flung into the arena to await the lions. She could not overlook the fact that women had been used by men for a very long time. If, as her grandfather seemed to be suggesting, she was in line for a large block of Maitland shares, her voting power would be an impressive asset. Men no less than woman saw no dishonesty in marrying for money.

They spent the next three hours very pleasantly together, and when Guy gauged it time to take their guest home, Antonia's expression was genuinely regretful.

'How the time has flown!' she exclaimed, and they both laughed at her expression. 'You probably think, Skye, I'd never run out of stories!'

'I've enjoyed myself very much.' Skye looked directly into the wide, shining eyes. 'You're a wonderful story teller, Mrs Reardon. You should write.'

'Do you know,' Antonia gazed back at her with obvious pleasure, 'I'd like to. I always wrote as a girl. Once, would you believe it, I wanted a career. But then I married and I had Julian and the children and many social demands.'

'So why don't you start now?' Skye asked, only half teasing. 'You've travelled widely, you've met a lot of famous, very interesting people, you know the world of big business and politics very well—too well, as you say. You should write a novel. Use your background to turn it into a bestseller.'

'It's a bit late, isn't it, my dear?' Antonia asked doubtfully. 'A lot of books I pick up these days are incredibly explicit.'

'Everything you didn't want to know,' Guy agreed with a slight smile.

'Tell it as you know and understand it,' Skye murmured. 'You said you're not happy with so much time on your hands, just as you're tired of so much of the old life. I think at this point, you should try something new.'

'It's certainly an idea.' Suddenly Antonia looked like a little girl, her large eyes filled with a bubbling excitement. 'As they say, life goes on, and we must go with it to the end. I thought I was at the beginning of old age. In fact, as I know you've noticed, I've suffered from a deep depression ever since my beloved Julian died. There didn't seem any point in anything.'

'You can't mean that, Tonia,' said Guy, and took his mother's hand. 'You know what you mean to *me*. And Adrienne.'

'With Adrienne, who knows?' Antonia answered a little bleakly. 'Sometimes I think I've lost my daughter, she's changed so much in the past few years.'

'All of us do a lot more thinking than is actually good for us.' Guy's dark, handsome face went hard. 'Adrienne has ... problems. We're aware of them. None of our dreams worked out, what we hoped for and expected, but it's a common crisis. How to make a new life?'

'It's easier when one is young,' Antonia said, speaking very slowly, with the remembrance of old pain.

'Clearly you're young enough, Tonia, to do a lot of living.' Guy drew his mother's fragile figure under his arm. 'You've told me many times you've wanted to write, and I distinctly recall Father's saying—"If you *want* to, you *will*, surely"?'

The most poignant expression settled upon Antonia's fine, delicate features. 'He did say that, didn't he? Julian always knew what he had to do and did it. That anyone could say he took his own life! He was probably working on some plan at the very moment. . . .' Her eyes filled with tears and Skye spontaneously stretched out her hand, clasping Antonia's with her own. She was no stranger to desolation herself, so she knew what Antonia was feeling, even if she didn't know the real facts concerning Julian Reardon's tragic death.

'My God, this is killing me,' Antonia groaned.

'It *isn't*,' Guy said harshly, 'because you know. You know what happened, Mother, was an accident. Father *was* thinking of other things but his driving. He was thinking of winning back the company—he never stopped thinking about it. And you. The whole world can gossip and say what they think. We know.'

'It's all right, Skye,' Antonia tried to smile. She could see now that the young girl beside her was deeply distressed. Even the fingers looped so comfortingly through her own were slightly trembling. 'I've invited you to dinner. We've had a lovely time, and now I've upset you.'

Skye shook her head. 'I don't like to see you so unhappy.'

'I don't want to be unhappy,' sighed Antonia. 'It's just that I don't seem able to handle loss. Julian was everything in the world to me. We were so happy. We had one another and the children. Julian was so proud of them. He always expected Guy to take after him. Boys are supposed to *be* something, aren't they, but he was absolutely thrilled when Adrienne turned out to be a high achiever. Julian was really a champion of women. He actually disliked anyone who wasn't. I

think he'd want me to do something with my life. I've
never been assertive, but writing a book isn't so
preposterous after all. I have a soul and a lot of
experience, of a sort.'

On the drive home, Skye was very quiet. 'What is
it?' Guy demanded.

'Nothing.' She turned her head, in reality feeling
very weak and vulnerable.

'My mother didn't mean to upset you, Skye.'

'No, of course not—I know that. In any case, I
wasn't thinking about myself. She looks so fragile, so
lost.'

'Five years ago you would have thought her
destroyed.'

'Those *eyes*!' she sighed.

'You don't know how beautiful she was before it all
happened. But she's not a strong woman, as you're
strong already. My father made all the decisions, all
the plans, always. Not because he swept everyone
along as your grandfather does, but because it was left
to him as his role. He would never, ever, have
willingly deserted my mother. No matter what anyone
might tell you, Skye, concerning my father's death and
the unresolved circumstances, he wasn't the type to
consider suicide as a way out. Responsibility,
commitment, was the very essence of his life. Neither
did he doubt his ability to carry on somehow. My
father was a brilliant man. At the same time he had
more principles than your grandfather.'

'That sounds cruel, Guy,' she said. 'Are you
suggesting that my grandfather is not completely
honest in his dealings?'

'I would expect your loyalty to him,' he said
bluntly, 'but a more profoundly ruthless business man
than your grandfather would be hard to imagine.'

'Then why sell out your own principles to work for
him?' Skye said heatedly.

'My father gave much of his life to Reardons,' he

said grimly. 'Perhaps he *gave* his life. In those last days there was no question he wasn't deeply disturbed. Your grandfather had been putting rumours about for months—he's a master of strategy, even the extreme ones, and Reardons' stocks had fallen to an all-time low. That was the time Maitlands launched their full attack. I've investigated this all very thoroughly, Skye, and I make no secret of the fact that I consider Sir Charles to be one of the all-time great pirates. When he suggested kindly that I come into the business, we both knew what we were doing. My father's mantle passed to me and Reardons retained enough clout for me to play at your grandfather's game. I'm not a better man than my father, I don't always behave impeccably, but I run no danger of being nailed to a wall.'

'And still Grandfather retains you knowing your view?'

The beautiful, chiselled mouth twisted. 'It's no longer a question of his retaining me, Skye, as you so disapprovingly put it. I'm much too valuable to him to let go.'

'You mean Uncle Justin and Warren are just rabbits?'

'Hey, did I say rabbits?' He glanced at her briefly. 'I told you when I first met you, you had Grandfather's aura.'

'You didn't mean it as a compliment.'

'Powerful people can cause an awful lot of pain,' she pointed out.

'Surely a bright little thing like you can look after yourself?'

'I guess so. Except now it's so new and strange and frightening.'

'Not stimulating?' Unquestionably there was mockery.

'Do you want my honest opinion, Guy?' she asked him.

'I'm all for it.' Instead of pulling into Huntingdon's driveway he brought the car to a halt in the narrow, tree-lined cul-de-sac.

'Aren't we going in?' Skye's voice trembled—a bad error.

'In a minute. I'm still waiting for your honest opinion.'

'I'm sure you know it already. My family have made you suffer. Now you're dangerous—you want revenge.'

'Surely you're not thinking *you* represent a unique opportunity to get it?'

'I don't think I come into it at all.'

They were alone together in the dark with the street lamps glowing like great golden fruit amid the boughs. A white moon rode serenely above the houses, trailing silver stars like streamers in the wind. It was a beautiful night, a beautiful, glittering night, the air flower-drenched and the devil himself beside her, darkly, mockingly, handsome and dangerous. It was so unnerving, Skye bit her lip hard.

'*Ouch!*' she exclaimed.

'Hurt yourself?' He stretched out his hand and turned her face towrds him. 'Don't want to tell me what it is?'

'This——' She touched a finger to her bottom lip. 'I think I bit too hard.'

'Show me.' Guy pressed the button for the interior light and Skye discovered dismayingly that his appalling attraction for her was even stronger in the soft light. Just his hand on the side of her face and her breath seemed to be shuddering in her body, her skin so sensitised the brush of his fingers was like a live wire. 'What a beautiful mouth you have, Skye.' His dark head came forward.

'Don't you kiss me,' she whispered.

'So why arch your head back?' His voice was hard and tight. 'I've been waiting to kiss you all night.'

'But I can't deal with it, Guy!'

'It might be easier if you shut your eyes.'

Her tongue came out unconsciously to moisten her mouth and he gave a low groan in his throat and reached for her, spearing his long fingers through her hair, curling her hair tightly, holding her face up to him as his mouth closed a little savagely over her parted lips.

Immediately she was on fire, at the mercy of the passions he aroused in her too easily. 'I want to be alone with you,' he muttered. 'Quite alone—not here.' One hand slid down over her shoulder and across her breast, cupping it swiftly from beneath, the thumb finding the peaked nipple through the warm, thin silk of her dress.

'No, Guy!' She put her hand over his. She had never felt so vulnerable, so much a *woman*, in her life.

But his mouth never left hers, neither did he shift that dominating hand.

She was feeling so much, the tears filled her eyes. He was so acceptable to her, it was terrifying. Instead of retaining her usual control and awareness, she was capitulating rapidly. She wanted him very badly, just as she knew he wanted it this way. Yet once he had had the chance to take her, to capitalise on this familiar, wild passion, and he had turned her away in shock.

'What a hell of a place to make love!' Finally he lifted his head.

Skye was shivering with reaction, her body so trembly she felt she wouldn't be able to stand. 'Agreed,' she said shakily, starting to push back her heavy fall of hair. 'You'd make the most marvellous lover, Guy, so I'm going to be very, very careful from now on.'

His silver eyes glittered. 'Are you frightened of relationships?'

'Oh, no.' His masculine fragrance was still in her

mouth and on her skin. 'Not relationships, but *you*. Obviously you're disgustingly attractive to me, much like one can get drunk on a certain wine. The answer is to seal oneself off from temptation.'

'I'll try to make it difficult for you.' He offered her a beautiful, comforting smile.

'Why?'

'*Really*, Skye!' From raw emotion he was back to the mockery. 'You're a perfectly beautiful girl in just the way that I like. You're spirited and tender and full of an enormous vitality. To be terribly candid, I'm in real fear of you. My life isn't exactly ordered, but I was working towards an established plan. Now you're here, and you're very desirable.'

'But a high risk?'

'Possibly.'

'Then you shouldn't have let any of ... this happen.'

He started laughing, a black, velvety sound in his throat.

'What's the joke?' she asked.

'I can't accept that I didn't *try*. I distinctly recall pressing you out of my room when I wanted you very badly. I think if you'd turned around you might have stayed. As it is, I think we're both bound to come to it. Inevitably.'

'As all women come to you?' She flicked a curl back from her temple.

'Not many, Skye.'

'Who are they?'

'Are you sure you want to know?' There was gleaming mockery in his eyes.

'Do we count Jo Anne?' she asked.

'I just happen to know Jo Anne very well,' he shrugged.

'Do you know that she's in love with you?'

'I suspect she thinks she is,' Guy admitted.

'Have you made love to her?'

'Let's get it over.'

'*Have* you?' Skye was quietly serious, not jealous or curious.

'I'm certain I've never kissed her like I've kissed you.'

'That must make you feel remarkably virtuous. Don't men still want to take a virgin bride to their bed?'

'I'm not so certain she *is* a virgin,' he said mildly. 'Few girls are.'

'I'm proof there are still a few left.'

'That's quite something, Skye.' He leaned forward, held up a lock of her hair and kissed her beneath the ear. 'You must have suffered intensely when you offered yourself to me so spontaneously.'

He had tilted her head back and now she looked up at him with burning eyes. 'You're going to relish that until you die!'

'You can get even if you like.' Now his finger traced the outline of her profile, lingering over the heat of her mouth. 'In the very short time I've known you I've admitted more to you than any other woman I know. I've even admitted I want you.'

She lay back quite still without turning her head. There was a delirium about this state, a curious floating. 'One needs time to believe in . . . emotions.'

'Yes, and I'll be gone for twelve days.'

'Oh—where?' His words even shook her heartbeats. It didn't seem possible a near stranger could be so firmly entrenched in the very fabric of her life.

'Japan. As no doubt you know, we do a lot of business with them.'

'Oh, well,' she produced a smile, 'I daresay I'll be very busy, and Jeremy is arriving.'

'I've known a couple of guys like Jeremy,' he said. 'They went to school with me, through university. Clever, good-looking, good at sports, yet there was never much there. You haven't heard if his mother is coming as well? It's funny what makes certain mothers run their sons' lives.'

'The fact they only have one another might have something to do with it,' Skye said.

'Anyway, Skye,' he pointed out mildly, 'she doesn't altogether approve of you. Perhaps it's a blessing really. I dread what might happen if she accepted your little affair with Jeremy as final. You'd be in a spot of bother trying to get away.'

'I never dreamed he would really come,' Skye sank further into the bucket seat.

'Perhaps a certain denseness enters into it,' Guy suggested. 'Are you sure you told him you'd outgrown him?'

'I feel sorry for him,' she said confusedly. 'Jeremy is my friend.'

'Women always fall back on "friend" when they don't want a lover. I'll bet Jeremy and his mother have sat down together and soberly ticked off your assets. Sir Charles Maitland's granddaughter. Naturally they'll think you've already got a bit of money....'

'I *have.*'

'I should hope so,' he returned dryly. 'You've never been properly provided for before. I can't think the rest of the family will have to go on rations.'

'I'd really like to talk about Adrienne and Warren,' said Skye. 'Absolutely no one thinks they're going to make a good team. I thought too that Adrienne didn't even like me.'

'Certainly she was being very thoroughly tested with Warren gaping at *you.*'

'You're *mad!*' It seemed unbearably sad.

'No, I'm not, little one. It must have registered with you. You and Warren have never lived together as cousins. To him, you're a ravishing stranger. It wouldn't take a genius to read my sister's thoughts. Although she'll deny it categorically I think she's marrying Warren to get Huntingdon back.'

'But that's crazy!'

'She's clever,' Guy shrugged. 'I didn't say she wasn't crazy. I like Warren. I've never paid much attention to him, but he seems to be decent and capable of backing up the generals. Given all the time in the world he'll never develop into a hard-headed business man, let alone a ferocious one, but I've found, too, he's good with people. People are important to Warren, not abstract ideas or systems. They should have put him into Personnel instead of pushing him into a job he doesn't really want to handle. I've had to take pity on him myself, he's been left so often to flounder. It seems odd that neither his grandfather nor his father had tried to help him. They just tossed him in, thinking automatically that he would swim.'

'He appreciates your help,' Skye said.

'I wish he'd think twice about marrying my sister,' Guy answered in his remotest voice. 'She's not in love with him.'

She turned her glowing head to look at him. 'And you? You're going to marry for love, are you, Guy?'

'Why do you say that as though it's so bizarre?' He caught a lock of her hair and tugged it none too gently.

'Oh, that hurt!' she gaped.

'I meant it to,' he said without hesitation. 'There's got to be a woman somewhere I can love.'

'Frankly I think you might put her through hell.'

'And why is that?' He drew her head still closer.

'That's precisely your image. You're like some superb, caged animal. You seem perfectly safe, yet you're the ultimate in danger.'

'Thank you,' he said a little angrily. 'Of course I am—to you.'

'Don't do it, Guy.' She was about to say something more, but his mouth came over her own again, starting off the soft, shuddering spirals that built up in her body. He was only kissing her, holding her head, yet the wealth of sensation was dizzying, in that moment, the pinnacle of intimacy.

My God, she thought wildly, even as she tore her mouth away, I'm in love with him . . . love with him. She didn't want it, this frightening pull. It was like being possessed.

'Okay,' his soft laugh was a little harsh. 'You're not the only one who's having problems. I don't like *your* effect on me either.'

There was a peculiar, very tense silence as they stared at each other, then Guy shrugged and started up the car.

CHAPTER SEVEN

SELLING the house and organising the removal of those things she wanted to keep was a painful episode for Skye. The realisation that she had truly lost her father was brought achingly home as she packed up clothing and books she knew would be appreciated by one of the charitable organisations. She cried so much she couldn't even see out of her eyes. Without meaning to she had found moments of happiness and excitement in the last weeks; now it seemed terribly wrong. She had wanted to mourn her father singlemindedly, yet her life was being swept up from her with such force. It was a terrible time of wrestling with her conscience. Her father had kept her deliberately from her grandfather, yet here she was acting as though none of it had happened. As though she and her grandfather had never been parted. As though her father had wanted this. Skye bowed her head into one of her father's shirts and sobbed. She couldn't bear to admit to herself how much she missed him ... that she had already begun to live her life.

When the phone rang she staggered up on almost useless limbs, her husky, 'Hello,' little more than a whisper.

It was Guy. Her breath drew in sharply as she recognised his voice. He sounded curt and anxious at one and the same time. 'I don't understand why you're there on your own,' he told her.

'Who would be with me?' she managed. 'Have you arrived back early or something?'

'Yes, I completed my business in record time.' It was obvious he sensed her desolation from hundreds of miles away. 'Surely Jo Anne could have gone with you? She has nothing to do.'

'Jo Anne and I aren't really close.' She spoke quietly with the same sadness she was feeling. 'Anyway, I wouldn't want to upset her. It *is* upsetting, you know.'

'I'm genuinely worried about you, Skye,' he told her.

'I know you are,' she gave a little shuddering sigh. 'But please don't be. I'm almost finished here.'

'You sound terrible.' His own voice was harsh.

'I miss him terribly, Guy. God. . . .'

'I can't get a bloody plane out of here,' he said tightly, 'it's too late. But I'll get the early one in the morning. I'll be with you for breakfast.'

'Oh, don't worry, Guy,' she cried, infinitely comforted even as she protested.

'How are you expected to handle it all on your own?' he countered grimly. 'You want to sell the house?'

'Yes.'

'No problem. You should have let me know what you intended to do.'

'I thought I could handle it,' Skye explained faintly.

'The strongest can't take it. It's well after nine, now. Why don't you go to bed?'

'I think I will.' She could see herself in the hall mirror, white-faced and swollen-eyed. 'Are you sure you're able to come?'

'See you in the morning, Skye,' Guy said crisply, and hung up.

She was waiting for him at the front door when he arrived in a taxi.

'Hi!' His voice was very gentle as he reached out and put an arm around her shoulder. He wasn't wearing one of his impeccably tailored business suits but beige slacks, an open-necked white shirt and a black wool-silk blazer. The effect was still very striking and Skye stood very still looking up at him. 'It's so . . . kind . . . of you to . . . come.'

He only shook his head. Although she had tried desperately not to cry all morning she was obviously still very much distressed. 'Had your breakfast yet?'

'No, I waited for you.' She didn't seem to have the strength to withdraw her fingers from his.

'I'll have to make a call, all right?'

'Of course.' Her violet eyes were uncertain. 'I hope you haven't made things difficult for yourself coming here?'

'Everything is just fine. You get the breakfast, then we'll go for a walk in that little park before we tick off what we have to do.'

A few moments later as Skye was working in the kitchen she heard him ask in a very business like voice to speak to a Mr Taylor, and as Mr Taylor came on the line, the tone became even more steely. She set the table quietly in the sunroom while the conversation went on for a full ten minutes.

'Problems?' She looked up as Guy approached her.

'Nothing I can't handle. Some people don't want to give you a jot more than what they're paid for. You can be certain they won't end up as management.'

'Shall I take your jacket?'

He was shouldering out of it, and Skye put out her hand.

'Thank you.' And then, as though unable to stop himself, he reached out and drew her gently into his arms. 'You've been tearing yourself to pieces, haven't you?'

She buried her face in the crook of his shoulder. 'Yes.'

'I don't understand how your family let you come on your own.'

'They're not my family, are they? In the real way.' *You're* more my family, she thought. How I feel actually matters to you.

'What did your grandfather say when you told him you were coming?' he asked.

'He realised I had to, of course.'

'But this is too much—sending you alone! My mother would have come with you, for that matter.'

'She's been through too much of a bad period herself.'

'Yet she's good when the people she cares about are troubled.'

Skye looked up at him then and he smoothed back her heavy hair with one hand. 'Do you think I really belong with Grandfather now?'

'You see it as a disloyalty to your father?'

'Yes.'

'It's *your* life, Skye,' he urged. 'You can't refuse to live it because of an old feud. There's no dishonour in having some love for your grandfather. You do care about him, don't you?'

'Yes, I do.'

'I think your father would understand. Any sort of relationship might have been impossible for him, but you don't have to atone for the past. Your grandfather loves you, wants you. It's hard to imagine how he let you go off on your own, but still. . . .'

'He told me he'll be waiting.'

'All right.' He smiled and shrugged. 'Can I take a chance on one of your breakfasts?'

'I'm a good cook.' Skye returned the smile and drew away shakily. 'I've done bacon and eggs.'

'Have you really?' Guy's silver eyes shone in the morning light.

'Sure. I had to make a special trip to the shop.'

By the end of the day Skye discovered his work pace was staggering. He told her he would organise everything and he did just that. She suddenly realised what qualities went into making these powerful individuals. The people he spoke to seemed to jump to attention as if to a challenge. The motivated agent brought four people to see the house and left a message late afternoon that he had drawn up a contract with a Mr and Mrs Wendell who had fallen immediately in love with the wonderful garden. Gardening was their passion, and Skye felt immense pleasure and relief that her father's garden seemed certain to be as loved and looked after as her father would have wished. Even the problem of the furniture was solved. The Wendells like a lot of what they saw and wished to buy it, while the rest they gave away to the neighbours who wandered in to say hello. Other things were packed professionally and dispatched in boxes to different, grateful organisations, and every time Skye looked like standing still at the front door, Guy directed her attention to a dozen other pressing matters.

By the end of the day, although she had really done very little, she was overcome.

'The kids were thrilled with that fridge!' Guy came in smiling. They had given the refrigerator away to the local church hall. 'God, you look sleepy!'

'Very sleepy.' Skye opened her half-closed eyes and smiled. 'You've done everything, Guy, and I've let it all go to hell.'

'A woman's *got* to need a man.' He slumped down beside her on one of the two remaining sofas. 'I'm damned pleased we've got someone to take care of the garden.'

'It was nice of them to come back.'

'I think they'd have bought the house, no matter what.'

'I'm glad,' said Skye.

'Well, we can't go home tonight and I suppose we'd better not stay here?' He turned his head and stared at her, eyes gleaming, sculptured mouth quirked.

'Do you really think you're irresistible?' she said wryly.

'I can hardly wait to find out!'

Her whole body was melting with the longing for him to take her into his arms. 'You forget how delicate my position is, Guy Reardon. All the neighbours know we're here. All of them invited us to their home. All of them were very taken with you, it's true, but there's still the thing, people like to talk.'

'Surely a trivial consideration against a thrilling night?'

'You sound as if you're teasing!'

'I am. You're exhausted.' Guy spoke in a firm quiet voice. 'We're going to lock up here, drop the key off and check into the Parkview for the night. I knew I couldn't talk you into a double room, so I've booked a room for both of us. You can take a shower to wake yourself up, then we'll have dinner.'

Jo Anne was livid when she found out Guy had rushed to her cousin's side.

'Don't get so uptight, darling,' Felicity cautioned her. 'You make it sound like a romantic assignation, when we all know Guy.'

'Know *Guy*?' Jo Anne looked as though she was ready to explode. 'Guy drives us all crazy, he's so damned unknowable!'

'What do you mean?' Felicity's handsome face tightened. 'He's very fond of you.'

'Sure. He's fond of me like a kid he's known for ever. I don't know if you're aware of it, Mamma, but he doesn't listen to a word I say.'

'You're an exceptionally attractive girl,' Felicity defended.

'Yes, but I can't reach him. Our interests aren't the same, as I keep reminding myself over and over.'

'I'm very sure, my dear, he doesn't want you to talk business,' said Felicity. 'He gets enough of that all day.'

'He still talks it in private,' Jo Anne maintained.

'Skye wants more from life than just being "an exceptionally attractive girl". God knows why, her face is her fortune.'

'Sky is too assertive, in my opinion,' Felicity said firmly. 'Mark my words, if she keeps up this career talk, she'll finish up an old maid. A man doesn't marry a competitor. He wants a woman who keeps herself and their home beautiful for when he walks in.'

'Why are you always talking about what the men want, Mamma?' Jo Anne glared at her mother strangely. 'Ever since I can remember it's been what Grandfather wants, or Daddy, and even Warren. I might find it reasonable to conclude that you don't give a damn about yourself. Or me. What the heck is our function, for God's sake?'

'I can see Skye has unsettled you,' Felicity's elegant face had turned white. '*I* am of enormous help to Grandfather. And to your father, of course. I may not advise them about any aspect of their business life, but I keep this house running smoothly.'

'You mean Nancy keeps it running!' Jo Anne shrieked. 'Nancy does all the work, but she doesn't get the recognition.'

'Nancy is only the housekeeper,' Felicity reminded her daughter coldly. 'I would not care to ask her to preside at the dinner table.'

'God, Mamma, you're a snob! Nancy's nice. It's our money that makes us different—Grandfather's money. In every real sense we're kept.'

'Women *are* kept by their men as a rule,' Felicity pointed out.

'I think someone threw the rule book out of the window.' Jo Anne poured Coca-cola into a glass and tossed it off ruthlessly. 'Why did no one ever care what *I* did?'

'In what way, darling?' Because Felicity loved her daughter she choked back her own anger.

'You know—school. There was never any talk about

what *I* was going to be. You and Daddy used to drive
yourself frantic about Warren's results, but you
weren't the least concerned about *me*!'

'But, darling, women have a different role.' There
was a look of sorrow on Felicity's face. 'There was no
need for you to make your own way.'

'I wish I wasn't born rich—like Skye,' said Jo Anne
bitterly.

'I'm sure Skye is happy to be Sir Charles Maitland's
granddaughter now,' Felicity returned acidly.

'Skye doesn't care about Grandfather's money,' Jo
Anne maintained. 'She seems to enjoy taking her
chances in a man's world. What I can't stand,' and
here tears filled Jo Anne's eyes, 'is Guy's wanting to
be with her. I'm so angry I can't see straight!'

'Yes, darling,' Felicity drew her daughter's glossy
head on to her shoulder. 'You just leave it all to me.
Now, I tell you what we'll do. I'll ring up a table at
Carlo's and we'll go to lunch.'

'I don't want lunch.'

'It doesn't matter, we're going. After that, we'll do a
little shopping. You ought to have a new mink jacket
for winter.'

Jo Anne nodded sadly. 'She needn't think she'll get
Guy. I'll never let it happen!'

There and then Felicity decided she had better
speak to Skye.

The occasion presented itself after dinner that night.
Jo Anne had been persuaded into going to the ballet,
Warren and Adrienne had gone off and the men were
full of some deal Guy had clinched, just like that.

'Walk in the garden with me, dear,' Felicity smiled.

'Love to. It's a glorious night.' Skye was a little
surprised Felicity had asked her, but she wasn't kept
wondering long.

'I gather Guy was a great help to you,' Felicity said,
breaking off a gardenia and twirling it under her nose.

'I shouldn't have been able to manage without him.'

'And you're such a naturally confident, resourceful girl.'

'I was feeling rather fragile yesterday,' Skye said.

'Of course,' Felicity responded hastily. But then she added: 'You quite like Guy, don't you?'

'It's difficult not to,' Skye exclaimed. 'He saved my life.'

'He *what*?' Felicity looked and sounded taken back completely.

'I was pretty distraught the day of my father's funeral and I rushed out on to the street. I really should have looked where I was going, because I was nearly collected by a car. Guy moved like lightning and threw me up on to the traffic island. In the end he even covered me with his own body. He's very brave.'

'Couldn't you have told us before?' Felicity challenged a little coldly.

'I'm sure he wouldn't want me to mention it,' explained Skye 'Even now. He called it nothing.'

'You're not in love with him, are you, Skye?' Felicity threw the gardenia away, asking sharply.

'I wouldn't want to be in love with Guy,' she evaded.

'That's no answer!'

'Surely I may be excused not answering, Felicity,' Skye said politely. 'After all, it is *my* business.'

'*Our* business too, my dear,' Felicity said hardily. 'You do realise Guy has given Jo Anne every reason to think he's very fond of her?'

'I imagine he would be. He's known her all her life.'

'You know very well what I mean!' Felicity sounded annoyed. 'It would be wrong of you to come between them.'

'Terribly wrong, if they were engaged or married, but they're not,' Skye pointed out.

'You're playing with fire, my dear,' Felicity said.

Skye hesitated, almost afraid to say it. 'Are you sure Jo Anne has read Guy's feelings correctly?' she asked.

'Do you mean is she living in endless hope?'

'Something like that.'

'Why do you ask, Skye?' Felicity challenged her directly. 'Has Guy been tempted to make love to you?'

'Sorry—you have to put me aside,' Skye countered. 'Do you really think Guy would see me or any other girl if he were in love with Jo Anne?'

'It's only too easy to divert a man's attention,' Felicity sighed. 'Your looks are stunning, Skye, you'll be hearing that regularly, but surely you realise you're hurting your cousin, inviting so much of Guy's attention. And I mean that. I feel you've capitalised on the situation—appealing to Guy to see you through when you could have managed quite easily on your own.'

'Nonsense!' Skye said shortly. 'This is where I draw the line, Felicity. I appreciate you feel you're speaking in Jo Anne's interests, but give me a chance to say one thing. I did *not* appeal to Guy to follow me. He came of his own accord. Probably I couldn't have stopped him. I don't want you to be angry with me and I don't want to hurt Jo Anne, but I think you should look at this again. It seems to me Guy is set against marriage.'

'Rubbish!' Felicity came to a halt, regarding Skye with some suspicion. 'All men complain that they get tricked into marriage, taking pleasure in the joke.'

'I don't think he loves Jo Anne,' Skye said gently. 'I know he thinks of her as someone special, but she may have to deal with the fact, that's all.'

'Obviously you've discussed it,' said Felicity, breathing hard.

'I'll admit I did ask him if he knew Jo Anne was in love with him.'

'And what did he say?'

'She only *thought* she was.'

'There you are!' Felicity exclaimed triumphantly. 'He's unsure of her.'

'Is that what you make of it?' asked Skye.

'Yes, of course. Well, it must be.' Once again Felicity began to move; past the circular fountain and the Gothic archway overgrown with a yellow flowering vine. 'Guy's such a mixture. He's so forceful, dynamic, but he really wants a woman who'll be subordinate to all that vitality. I really can't understand, my dear, why you're pestering Grandfather for a job?'

'Good heavens, Felicity, I need one!' protested Skye.

'But *why*?' Felicity sounded genuinely astonished. 'As I understand it, Grandfather has already made you financially secure.'

'Certainly he has,' Skye nodded, 'but I've had the training to do a certain job. I need to use my abilities.'

'My dear girl, career women suffer a real loss of their femininity!'

'You can't believe that, Felicity,' Skye looked at the older woman unhappily.

'Not only believe it, I've seen it—many times. In addition, I've seen a great deal more than you. Why, Grandfather wouldn't take on a woman as a business partner. We really can't be relied on.'

'That's precisely what we *can* be,' Skye retorted, determined not to get angry. 'Women are very heavily relied on. You're mistress of a very large home, you're Grandfather's hostess. He relies on you in those capacities.'

'Of course—the womanly things. Men and women have a different role to play. And Skye,' Felicity turned to her urgently, 'I would ask you to stop putting your revolutionary ideas into Jo Anne's head. This feminist business has my sympathy up to a point, but I won't have my daughter unsettled just because she's not out there clawing her way to the top.'

*

It was pouring with rain the day Jeremy arrived in Sydney, and by the time they reached the car, Skye's hair was curling wildly in the damp, humid conditions.

'It's splendid of you, darling, to meet me.' Jeremy gave her a grateful, loving glance not unmixed with a little shock. In the weeks since he had seen her, she seemed to have undergone some important change. Before, her beauty had been understated; now she seemed to be revelling in it. It was difficult for him to uncross his eyes.

'Listen—as we're friends, Grandfather said you can stay with us for a day or two until you find your own place. That will give you today and tomorrow, plus the weekend.'

'I say, I never expected such hospitality. Thank you—that's very kind.'

'How's your mother?' Skye asked.

'A little tremulous,' Jeremy said reservedly, 'but she'll come round. She saw me off.'

'Well, Sydney's only an hour away.'

'She doesn't like planes. Every trip is going to be fatal—that kind of thing.'

'Then you'll have to write her.'

'Speaking of writing,' Jeremy glanced at her, 'I didn't hear much from you.'

'Actually I recall writing to you twice.' Skye braked abruptly as an elderly woman stepped right out on to the road to hail a taxi.

'My goodness, she won't last long!' Jeremy stared back through the outside mirror. 'Why do people act twice as stupidly in the rain?'

'Probably they have to catch a cab, they can't walk.'

'You look very beautiful, Skye,' Jeremy said quietly. 'Your new environment has worked on you already. You look like some gorgeous jungle cat.'

'*Jungle cat*?' she repeated with a little laugh. 'That's

an unexpected compliment. Then again, it's the strangest thing, but people used to call Grandfather a lion on the loose. I think it must have something to do with a fiery mane.'

'You certainly look exotic.'

Skye glanced at him briefly, realising he wasn't altogether happy with her new image. She wasn't particularly aware of it, but she did look stunning. Her silk wrap-around dress was butter yellow and around her narrow waist she wore a wide, supple cummerbund of iridescent bronze. Her choker necklace was gold, and so were the earrings that set off her colouring to perfection.

'Was it because of *me*, Jeremy, you applied for this job?'

His smooth, good-looking face registered astonishment. 'I should think you'd realise that without asking.'

'I see.' Skye exhaled jerkily. 'I don't love you, Jeremy. I gave you an honest answer.'

'It's hard for me to believe you when we were so very close.'

'I've changed, Jeremy,' she said. 'It's all over.'

'For God's sake, Skye, I *love* you!' he protested.

'I'm sorry.' She drove, violet eyes looking straight ahead.

'You've been through a good deal, Skye. I understand.'

'Please, Jeremy,' she said softly, 'you have to give me up.'

'I should. You're so difficult to understand.'

'Don't let's quarrel.' She drive for a while in frowning silence. 'I told you how I felt, Jeremy, before I left.'

'I didn't really believe you knew what you were saying.' Jeremy looked at her with stricken eyes. 'What's happened, Skye? Only a short time ago you were ready to become my wife.'

'No, no, we never got that far!' she protested.

'All right, then, you felt a real commitment.'

'I cared about you, Jeremy—I still do. You're a very nice person.'

'God, what a cop-out!' There was anger and confusion in Jeremy's face. 'I can tell you the very day you began to change.'

'Okay then, tell me.'

'The day you met Reardon.'

'You mean the day of the funeral?'

'It was a special and terrible day.'

'It was the worst day of my life,' Skye said quietly.

'Darling, forgive me.' Jeremy reached out and brushed her cheek with one hand. 'All we've got to do is give it time and things will be the same again. Your system has had a terrible shock.'

'I can't allow you to hope, Jeremy,' she said unhappily. 'I made no promises.'

'I know you will eventually,' Jeremy answered in his most stubborn voice. 'And while I'm here, I'll give you some good advice. Leave Reardon alone. Men like that are capable of anything.'

'Explain!' she said fiercely.

'I don't have to. You know yourself. You may imagine yourself infatuated with him, but disillusionment can't be far behind. I've heard he's been involved with a lot of women.'

'Dare I ask your sources?' Skye was getting so angry she was driving too fast.

'And another thing! He's a goddamned hypocrite. How can he conceivably work for your grandfather when he must hate him?'

'He doesn't hate him,' Skye said coldly.

'Want to bet?'

'Not interested.'

'So you say,' Jeremy returned bleakly. 'I think you fell for him on sight.'

'I couldn't possibly!'

'It's true. God, darling, don't feel I don't understand. I'll bet he's well accustomed to having women fall for him. He looks like one of these damned heroes out of some fool romance—light eyes contrast strikingly with black hair and black brows. Women have been known to go frantic for less.'

'We'll soon be home,' Skye said tightly. 'Let's not talk any more about it.'

Jo Anne took a fancy to Jeremy at once.

'He's *very* nice!' she told Skye later, in some surprise. 'I've always liked fair men.'

'They don't come any darker than Guy.'

'Guy looks dangerous, though, doesn't he? Sort of a lot for any woman to handle. Your Jeremy looks easy to love.'

'He's not my Jeremy, Jo Anne,' said Skye, and walked to the great carved armoire to hang up her dress.

Jo Anne looked incredulous. 'He certainly thinks he is!'

'To the best of my knowledge I never once said I loved him.'

'Obviously he assumed you did.'

'You're right.' Skye stared at the floor thoughtfully. 'I detest hurting people.'

'One would never think so,' Jo Anne answered coolly. 'You're a whole new girl, you know, from when you first came here.'

'I don't think so.' Skye shook her head with a firm smile. 'I'm pretty much the same.'

'You don't seem to be aware of it, but all your new clothes have wrought a change. They'll be introducing *me* soon as Skye's cousin!'

'You'd outshine me any day,' Skye assured her.

It was said so earnestly, yet carelessly, Jo Anne had to laugh. 'You have no vanity, have you?'

'I don't even think about it.' Skye pulled out her

dress for the morning and held it against her.
'Businesslike enough?' She looked at Jo Anne
carefully.

'For what?'

'I'm going in to the office in the morning. I have to
show a couple of people an idea of mine.'

'Is this this new plant thing at Smithfield?'

'Yes.'

Jo Anne looked at her with dark, pitying eyes. 'I'm
afraid no one will take any notice of you, Skye. They
might pretend to so they won't offend Grandfather,
but there's no possibility that they'll listen to what you
have to say.'

'I won't say much—I'll just *show* them. They have
to make some attempt to create a good image. People
tend to worry when they're kept in the dark. It's up to
companies to let them know what they're doing when
they're building at the back door.'

'You get satisfaction from this, do you?' Jo Anne
asked.

'It's what I was trained for,' Skye reminded her.
'I'm good at my job.'

'Maybe,' Jo Anne jumped up from the armchair.
'But you won't get far inside Maitlands. It's an all-
male executive. You're just a little girl and un-
comfortably good-looking. I'd say that alone was a
massive handicap.' At the door Jo Anne turned her
head and gave Skye a quick glance. 'I thought Jeremy
was looking for an apartment in the morning?'

'He did say that,' Skye nodded.

'Aren't you going to go with him?'

'He'll be okay.'

'But he doesn't know Sydney well.' Jo Anne's eyes
were bright and questioning.

'Well enough.' Skye brushed her hair back with her
hand. 'Would you like to go with him?'

'I may as well.' Jo Anne put her hand on the door
handle. 'I have nothing else to do.'

'I know he'll appreciate it,' said Skye.

'He must be pretty bright,' Jo Anne said, halfway out the door. 'He'd never have been accepted otherwise.'

'Why, yes,' Skye's blue-violet eyes lit up as she smiled, 'I know he was very highly thought of at Strang's.'

'I think I know an apartment block that might suit him.' Jo Anne stopped and adjusted a painting that was hanging right outside the door. 'Might as well take him there first.'

'Good, he's used to a comfortable life.'

'By the way,' Jo Anne glanced at her watch, 'did you know dear Adrienne is dropping in tonight?'

'No, I didn't.'

'In that case,' Jo Anne smiled, faintly maliciously, 'be on your guard. She doesn't like the way you're turning poor old Warren's head.'

'Warren,' Skye replied without hesitation, 'is my cousin.'

'I don't think it's sunk in,' Jo Anne laughed shortly. 'He's full of a very uncousinly love and admiration!'

'I wish you wouldn't say that, Jo Anne,' Skye protested. 'Suggestion can be quite powerful.'

'I agree. But no one had to suggest anything to Warren. He was dazzled at first sight.'

'And you think Adrienne is aware of it?'

'My dear Skye,' Jo Anne drew in a short, urgent breath, 'Adrienne, like Guy, is almost shockingly acute!'

'She hasn't got his charm,' Skye ventured.

'I'll say she hasn't!' Jo Anne gave a little, bitter laugh. 'She's a loner, terribly distant. I believe at one point after her father ... died, she was suicidally depressed. I always think these too-intelligent types can be awfully unstable.'

'It must have come as an appalling shock to them all,' Skye said compassionately. 'You haven't had to

handle grief yet, Jo Anne, and I hope you don't have
to for a long time.'

'I remember when Grandfather had his first heart
attack,' Jo Anne said readily. 'You should have seen
the devastation around here! We all got such a terrible
fright, it was left to Guy to do everything. Daddy went
absolutely to the pack. I never believed he even loved
Grandfather until then—if that was even the reason.
Some people don't have the head to wear the crown. I
guess Grandfather is really a genius. He seems
gigantic to the rest of us, anyway.'

Sir Charles and Justin were dining with colleagues
that evening so the young people more or less had the
house to themselves. Jeremy, in such grand surroundings, had come alight, his conversation so engrossing
Jo Anne scarcely looked away from him. All through
dinner she leaned forward, dark eyes wide as Jeremy,
so encouraged, kept up a constant stream of amusing,
interesting, pleasant talk. The sort of talk she had
always wanted; not issues and profundities and
matters far removed from the pleasant, sociable life.
Jeremy didn't use terms and expressions that fazed
her. He didn't talk about inflation and unemployment,
the modus operandi of fiscal monetary policy, multi-
nationalism and overseas control of natural resources.
He was lively and entertaining, and he made them all
laugh a lot. Even Adrienne, so icily attractive, was
seen to smile. It seemed obvious, too, that Warren
found him pleasant company, to the extent of
organising eighteen holes on Sunday. It was then that
Adrienne pointed out that she had planned something
else, so to avoid disappointing Jeremy, Jo Anne, who
was a natural athlete, invited Jeremy to join her early
morning.

'It gets so terribly hot, even the best of us start to
peter out,' she explained.

When they withdrew to the library for coffee and
the liqueurs Warren dispensed so liberally, Jeremy

still had plenty of things to talk about. He settled his coffee on his knee and began to speak about a well known personality who had been jailed.

'Your friend is a great success.' Adrienne moved to sit beside Skye, her expression mildly derisive. 'I never realised he was such delightful company.'

'You go your way and I go mine. He's really not your type. So often we become involved with people who are not necessary to us.'

'True.' Skye glanced back at her directly. 'Are you assuming I'm involved with Jeremy?'

'Not at all. Not now. I don't think you would overcome a man with your attention unless he had something really interesting to say. On the other, Jo Anne just loves to talk trivia.'

'Don't be so highbrow,' Skye said mildly. 'We each relax in our own way. You, I think, don't relax at all.'

'How perceptive!' Adrienne appeared to find this genuinely amusing.

'It's a pity,' Skye said. 'It will cost you.'

'I know that.' There was acute misery at the back of Adrienne's fine eyes. 'I keep waiting for my mood to swing, but the pendulum got tied up.'

'Oughtn't you see a doctor?' Skye saw the tremble in Adrienne's slender ivory hands.

'A psychiatrist, you mean?'

'Someone you can talk to as much as someone who can prescribe something. You've been through a devastating time.'

'Hell,' Adrienne said quietly.

'So you know you need help to restore your inner self.'

'So who's going to help me?' Adrienne asked expressionlessly.

Before the older girl reverted to her freezing self, Skye wanted to give it a try. 'Forgive me, Adrienne, if I seem to be speaking out of turn, but you're not moving towards the people who love you most. Your mother needs you just as you need her. I would give anything for that loving-needing relationship. You've got it. You've got a brother—a man I know is like a rock in a crisis. Why would you turn your back on him? They, too, have been through hell, as you put it.'

'They're stronger than I am. Even Mother.'

'Then don't you feel you should be helping her? There's nothing in life that's not the better for sharing. We can't do well enough on our own. We need people to care for us, people to care *for*. Your mother misses your company, Adrienne. Guy wants his sister.'

'And you—how do you know so much?' Adrienne spoke curtly.

'I understand despair.'

'Yes.' Adrienne's eyes fell before Skye's. 'I believe you adored your father, yet you're surviving.'

'We all have to rebuild our lives, Adrienne, which is not to say we can discard the sadness. That remains. My father would be deeply disappointed in me if I failed to take hold of life again, if I failed to take pleasure in it. The people who love us want us to be happy. I've got to function again. Adrienne, shape my life the way we both planned it.'

'My father had great plans for me,' Adrienne said. 'I don't claim to be as brilliant as Guy, but I've come a long way.'

'I'm sure you're truly exceptional,' Skye told her. 'Science wasn't my area of expertise.'

'You realise I'm in the middle of a highly unpleasant situation at the moment, don't you?'

'No.' Skye looked at her questioningly.

'Your Uncle Justin. . . .'

'Your mean *your* fiancé's father?'

'Don't make matters worse. . . . Warren's father is doing his damnedest to block me in every step of my career.'

'You're sure of it, Adrienne?'

'Yes, of course.' The answer was bleak and uncompromising.

'Isn't there *anything* you can do?'

'Justin Maitland is a very influential man. And when he can't use his influence, he just pays them.'

'But that's terrible!' exclaimed Skye.

'It's bad. One of these days Guy will fix him—I mean really fix him. They killed my father.'

'Oh, *please*, Adrienne!' Skye covered the thin, trembling hands with her own. 'You'll never feel better if you bottle up so much rage.'

'It's so destructive, isn't it?' Adrienne agreed flatly.

'Fatal when one's thought are focusing on it all the time. Why are you engaged to Warren?'

'I love him.'

'You said that so oddly,' said Skye. 'I'm fond of Warren.'

'And he's embarrassingly fond of you.'

'You don't have to worry about me,' Skye told her.

'Maybe I'm like Guy,' Adrienne said. 'I'm playing my own hand.'

'Even if you hurt Warren who seems to have no bad tendencies.'

'How can I hurt him?' Adrienne demanded. 'Warren is prepared to settle down with me because his grandfather wants it! He has never made a decision in his whole life.'

'And you could marry a man you despise?'

'I care about him at the same time.' An ironic smile crossed Adrienne's pale ivory face. 'He's so unexpectedly nice for this family.'

'You don't like me either?'

'I can't think of a thing, Skye, that's not to your credit. Your father could be proud of you. He reared you with complete success.'

'Wouldn't *your* father want to say the same of you?'

Adrienne's small teeth bit into her bottom lip, but she didn't answer.

Jeremy refused to be ignored any longer. 'Skye!' he called imperatively.

'Yes, Jeremy?'

'I was telling these two about the time I was nearly taken by a crocodile, and they don't believe me.'

'But it's perfectly true.'

'I don't believe it!' Jo Anne laughed. She was looking radiant, the very picture of carefree youth.

Adrienne made a soft, scornful comment behind Skye's back, and Skye groped for her hand to hush her. Of course Jeremy had deserved his good fright, but he wouldn't have been all that indigestible for breakfast. 'The fact is,' she explained pleasantly, 'Jeremy had been warned not to go near the water. Not to paddle, much less swim. . . .'

'My God, it really happened!' Jo Anne put out her hand and grasped Jeremy's shoulder.

'I've always wanted to go to the Territory,' Warren said.

'It's fascinating, you've no idea!' Jeremy's fair, neat-featured face was unaccustomedly alive. 'Absolutely alive with wildlife! Probably the last great frontier. Anyway, we were out in the billabong country, that's the safari country proper, dotted with buffalo, you know. Rain hadn't fallen for months and it was appallingly hot. Honestly, I don't think you can beat this for real terror. . . .'

'He's off again,' Adrienne whispered wryly, but when Skye turned to look at her, for the first time ever, she saw a true smile in the lake-coloured eyes.

'Of course I thought it was a log,' Jeremy was saying to his enthralled audience. 'I mean, it was just floating like a log. I was more interested in looking at the birds. Birds, birds, birds. Millions of them everywhere. The brolgas! What a fantastic sight. . . .'

'Devil take the brolgas,' Adrienne said. 'Tell us about the man-eater with the big teeth!'

CHAPTER EIGHT

IF Skye was hoping to make a good impression on her Uncle Justin and his colleagues, she was doomed to frustration. They looked cautiously at sheet after sheet of proposed suggestions, complimented her smoothly and in the end said absolutely—nothing.

Somehow she managed to keep her own mouth shut until she was left alone in the boardroom with the man who was quite unlike his father, or Skye, for that matter.

'Well, what do you think, *really*?' she asked urgently.

'You've done a lot of work, my dear. What do we owe you?'

'An answer, I think.'

'Do you think so?'

'Surely, Uncle Justin.'

'You're very direct, aren't you, Skye?' He stared at her.

'Surely it would waste a lot of time to beat senselessly about the bush?'

'I still can't believe you're Deborah's daughter, you're so unlike her.'

'I thought I was supposed to be the image of her?' Skye said.

'To look at, yes.' He was still staring at her with eyes that didn't see. 'But your mother would have been almost ... colourless, beside you. No, my dear, you're more like your grandfather. You have the same kind of vigour. Everything has to be done without delay. Lights flashing on and off.'

'I guess that's how it is when one works hard.'

'My dear, you're only a child!' He turned slowly away from her.

'I appreciate that I haven't got a great deal of experience, Uncle Justin.'

'No, you haven't.' He moved to the bar, took down a bottle of whisky, poured some into a cut-glass tumbler and proceeded to swallow it. It was exactly ten-thirty.

'Would you have a mineral water?' she asked.

'I'm sorry, my dear.' He turned around to her as though he suddenly remembered she was there. 'Of course. I want to thank you, Skye, for your hard work on our behalf, but I can't see how we can possibly use your ideas. They're not really necessary, for one thing. People always mumble, but they soon settle down.'

'I think it would be a nice and smart gesture of Maitlands to retain, if not me, Public Relations on this thing,' said Skye. 'I have ideas, but I know I'm only a beginner.'

'You're surprisingly professional.' Justin Maitland took his glassess off and began to polish them. Without the heavy cover-up, his face looked rather shockingly naked and vulnerable.

'I wonder if Grandfather should look at it?' Skye ventured. She dared not say Guy.

'You knew how very busy Grandfather is with the Hammerford bid.'

'And you don't want to show him?'

'My dear girl,' Justin Maitland groped for his glasses and thrust them back on his nose, 'this may seem important to you, but my father is a very busy man, can't you understand? You may want to be a part of it all, but the idea is laughable. I don't want to hurt your feelings, but good God, you're only a kid of what . . . twenty-two?'

'Almost twenty-three.' Skye had a moment of acute upset and disappointment. 'May I remind you, Uncle Justin, that Grandfather made a fortune when he was still a kid in his twenties.'

'I doubt you could do the same,' Justin Maitland said very dryly.

'There's no real reason why I couldn't be a success.'

Justin Maitland smiled and picked up the telephone. 'Let me do you a big favour, Skye. Put the thought of making a career with Maitlands out of your mind. We can hand-pick our people, and they're rarely women.'

'I thought Mr Barlow looked impressed with the layout. In fact, Mr Morrison beside him couldn't hide his interest, only they take their position from you.'

'My dear,' Justin Maitland said kindly, 'you're right out of your depth. I know you mean well and I daresay we could trust you with something or other, but we simply don't need the sort of thing you've cooked up.'

'Okay,' Skye said abruptly, and began to roll up her work. 'It seems very short-sighted to me to let both sides fight it out when it could all be handled so much better. The field of Public Relations is expanding rapidly. I find it odd you don't see the value.'

She was still steaming by the time she reached the lobby, head down, not glancing from right to left.

'Skye!' a voice called to her. Guy and one of his aides had just walked into the building.

'Oh, hello there.' She smiled at the other man, who nodded pleasantly, half saluted Guy and went on his way.

'What's up?' Guy gave her one of his penetrating looks.

'Oh, I've been knocked back with my little project.'

'I see.'

'I know I'm supposed to love Uncle Justin, but I think I hate him,' Skye said wearily.

'It is confusing, isn't it?' Guy responded poker-faced.

'Is it because I'm a woman?'

'Very politely—yes. I think your uncle thinks

women make for chaos. Of course, he's been unhappily married for years.'

'Has he?' Skye was diverted.

'You didn't know he was unhappy?'

'I thought he was concealing something,' Skye said wryly. 'I can't keep this up, Guy. I have to move out of Huntingdon. I have to be independent of them all. Grandfather will just have to understand!'

'I suppose so.'

'You're not objecting?'

'No, I want to get you alone.' There was a teasing look around his eyes.

'But you were the one who brought me here!'

'So I was.' His handsome face sobered. 'I wanted you to have what what due to you—for your mother's sake. My clear recollection of her isn't in the least feigned. I'd have thrown myself at her feet, she was so beautiful and sweetness itself to an absurd little boy.'

'I think you must have been a very nice little boy,' Skye told him.

'Thank you.'

They seemed to be staring at one another intensely, neither smiling but with very serious expressions. Guy was the first one to break the spell. 'Want to come up to my office and show me?'

'I'd like your opinion.' Skye didn't falter.

They moved towards the descending lift and minutes later Guy's secretary, a very attractive woman in her late thirties, showed them into the office. 'What about coffee?' she smiled at them from the doorway.

'I'd love it,' Skye said in answer.

'Thanks, Janet.' Guy cleared a space of his desk. 'Hold my calls for about an hour.'

In fact they talked for the next two hours. 'Maitlands can't really offer you what you want to do, Skye,' he told her. 'You should look to one of the big agencies. Obviously you have ability. You can handle a major project on your own.'

'James taught me the ropes,' she explained.

'And he did his job well. Perhaps I could have a word with Bart Brophy.'

'Brophy and Howell?' Skye's tone expressed her respect for this most prestigious firm. 'Would he accept me?'

'He has no bias towards women.'

'I didn't mean that exactly. I'm very junior.'

'So were we all when we started, but you're capable of this.' He wound up the sheets. 'I'll keep these, if you don't mind.'

'I don't mind,' she said. 'It's a pity some of my ideas can't be used.'

'Oh, they'll be used all right,' Guy promised her.

'But you'll come into conflict with Uncle Justin.'

'Yeah, I guess so.' He seemed totally unconcerned. 'He ought to be so proud of you he'd show these to everyone around.'

'Maybe he really doesn't think it worthwhile,' she shrugged.

'He doesn't always see what's good for the business,' Guy said pleasantly. 'Now I'm going to tell you something you'll like to hear. I called in on Tonia after I left the office last night—and guess what she was doing?'

'Not writing?' Skye looked up at him, all soft attention.

'She was just sitting there typing, surrounded by at least fifty finished sheets. A veritable welter of inspiration!'

'So what's it about?'

'She wouldn't tell me.'

'How did she look?' Skye wanted to know.

'Excited. Stimulated. Anything but defeated.'

'But that's wonderful, Guy!' She gave him an expressive smile.

'I suppose I shouldn't have told you—it might spoil

your surprise. You *are* having lunch together next week?'

'Yes—Wednesday. Don't worry, it will be easy to look thrilled.'

'Like this?' He caught her face in his hands. There was a tremendous energy about him that was apparent even when he was quite still. Skye wanted to slide her arms around his neck, but all the while she was fighting it.

'Too dangerous,' she murmured, her violet eyes half closing.

'You don't think we could just enjoy each other without paying the consequences?'

'No,' she said softly, rather fiercely. 'I don't want to be another one of your women.'

'*My* women? Hey now!' Guy's silver eyes flashed.

She was about to answer him when the office door suddenly opened and a familiar voice said coldly: 'Oh, excuse me, Guy.'

They both turned around to face Justin Maitland fully. Behind him Janet Powell was pulling funny little faces suggesting apology and the need to excuse herself of all blame.

'Still here, Skye?' he asked shortly, and shut the door.

'Is there something you want, Justin?' The civilised veneer was so thin Skye went cold in reaction.

'Some very important documents have been removed from the files. It's a fair bet you've got them.'

'What documents?' Guy's tone was steely.

'This is private, Skye, do you mind?' her uncle said pointedly.

'I was just going.' She picked up her handbag and walked towards the door. 'I'll be hearing from you, Guy, shall I?'

His expression showed quite clearly his controlled anger. 'Depend on it.'

'That's something I've learnt about you,' she said.
'I *can*.'

Over the next month, a lot of changes took place. Skye
had her interview with Brophy and Howell and was
accepted on their staff. As a direct result a lot of her
ideas were incorporated into a highly successful public
relations programme for the Maitland Corporation.
Skye was given credit, a quick promotion, and best of
all Guy, despite minimal but powerful resistance, was
able to push the programme through.

Jeremy had become a very welcome visitor to the
house. These days he presented a very much more
sophisticated image, and although he was still refusing
to see Skye as out of reach, he plainly enjoyed Jo
Anne's company and there was no doubt she had
become deeply interested in his career. So interested
she had already taken Skye to task for her own
'militant ambitions' with only the 'odd word here or
there' for Jeremy. She herself was bending over
backwards to make up for Skye's failure.

'Mark my words, you'll lose him,' she often said.

If it were only that easy! Jeremy obstinately refused
to see that he and Skye were no longer a couple. He
was hideously jealous of Guy Reardon when Skye, for
her own reasons, did her best not to see him. Not that
Guy seemed to care. When it became apparent that
Skye was keeping him at arm's length, he devoted his
considerable talents to miffing her every time they
met. Her friendship with Antonia had progressed to a
much looked-forward-to weekly lunch date, but she
was plainly retreating from any involvement with
Antonia's son. It was a strange state of affairs, because
it took all her will power to avoid him and refuse the
invitations he offered in a very amused sort of way.
Skye had the horrible feeling he knew what she was
doing, but she wouldn't get far. There was even a
female logic in the perversity of her actions. If just the

sight of him made her catch her breath, she didn't dare speculate on just what might happen if she had dinner at his place. She had almost run out of good excuses.

Brophy and Howell kept her extremely well occupied, so she had to leap up from her desk to keep her weekly luncheon appointment with Antonia. To make it worse she was detained by a colleague before she made it to the front door; she missed a passing bus, and the restaurant was two blocks up the street.

'Sorry I'm late,' she apologised breathlessly.

'Oh, I'm glad to see you, dear.' Antonia looked up with a quick smile. 'You don't have to hurry like that, you know.'

'Out of breath!' Skye sank into the seat opposite. 'I can be back a little late.'

'And how's it going?' Antonia viewed the girl opposite her with pleasure. She wore a simply styled, beautifully cut black and white silk dress, good pearls in her ears and at her throat, shoes and handbag were black and she personified the kind of young woman, bright, generous, sensitive yet self-confident, that Antonia had wanted to be. 'You look so alive—as though the adrenalin is really flowing through your blood.'

'They keep me busy,' Skye smiled. 'Boy, I can't complain that I'm not using my potential! It's go, go, go. Soon as I think it's going to level off, Dave slaps some more work on my desk. But the rewards are there, Tonia, and the best thing of all is, they take me seriously.'

'What are you working on right now?' asked Antonia.

'A total switch—political liaison. Dave thinks I should do it. The time I spend reading, research. . . .'

'Well, what are you going have?'

'To start. . . .' Skye looked down at the menu with pleasure. 'You've no idea, I'm *starving*!'

Halfway through the meal Antonia delivered her news. 'Adrienne had dinner with me last night.'

Skye nodded. 'How is she?' Adrienne and she might never achieve the sort of relationship she had with Antonia, but there was more warmth lately on Adrienne's side.

'Hold hard! She's breaking off her engagement.'

Skye stopped eating and put her knife and fork down. All she could detect in Antonia's delicate, unlined face was a marked relief. 'Good!' she said.

Antonia looked a shade rueful. 'That's what *I* think. Thank God Warren won't be too hurt, and it was always a mystery to me why Adrienne got engaged to him in the first place.'

'And what was her attitude when she told you last night?' Skye studied the older woman quietly.

'Why,' Antonia's shining eyes suddenly misted with tears, 'she looked at peace. No pangs of regret. In fact, wishing she'd done it before. I knew the moment I opened the door.'

'She wanted to share it with you, didn't she?' Skye put out her hand and covered Antonia's with her own.

'It was like having the old Adrienne back.'

Skye smiled at her then. 'It seems as though Adrienne is finding herself again.'

'I want you to know something, Skye.' There was a little catch in Antonia's soft voice. 'You've been a godsend to my family.'

'Oh, Tonia, not at all.' A blush mantled Skye's creamy cheeks. 'Whatever have *I* done?'

'You've set an example.'

'No!'

'Yes, you have. You've made Adrienne and me see that no matter what our suffering there's still a richness in life. That it's still worth going on. That we must sublimate our grief.'

The sincerity in her voice was plainly apparent, and Skye, touched but disbelieving spoke very gently. 'It's a beautiful compliment, Tonia, but I don't deserve it.'

'I think you do, and so does Adrienne. I know she hasn't said much to you, but she's been observing. You're such a vital person, Skye, yet you're so caring. You're going to make a lovely, strong woman.'

'Not really,' Skye's quick, radiant smile returned. 'I'm terrified of your son.'

'He's terrified of *you*.' Antonia smiled softly.

'So each of us troubles the other.'

'I wonder why?' Antonia leaned across the table and picked up the salt. 'I know you're avoiding him intentionally, but I would like you to come with us to the beach house for the weekend.'

'Oh, Tonia!' Skye's violet eyes went wide.

'Guy said pretty much the same thing. Maybe more.'

'I'll bet! He has a very acid tongue. Just the three of us?'

Antonia sat smiling like a relaxed, happy child. 'Do you think we'd better ask a few more people along?'

'Jo Anne, I know, will be very put out if *I* get the invitation,' Skye pointed out.

'You know, I'm not terribly fond of Jo Anne, though she seems ... *softer* these days,' confessed Antonia. 'I've considered that angle, of course. . . .'

'Then again, I've committed myself to seeing Warren. Yet another confrontation. He won't take no for an answer.'

'Well, how about inviting them?' There was a spark of mischief in Antonia's eyes.

'You're up to something, aren't you?' said Skye.

'Good lord, no. It's just that it should be a heavenly weekend and you've never seen the place.'

'Can't Adrienne come?'

Antonia hesitated for a moment, then she blushed. 'I think there's some new man in her life.'

'Already?' Skye shook her head.

'She's mentioned him once or twice. She used to work for him at McQueens, only he left to set up his own company. Adrienne thinks he's destined for great things.'

'Oh!' Skye made quite a production of a simple monosyllable.

'She'd have to find someone of her own intellectual calibre,' Antonia ventured.

'Hmm, and I'll bet he's quite liberally endowed with the less spiritual qualities—not that it did poor Warren any good,' Skye sighed.

'I thought he was in love with you,' Antonia said with a certain mild teasing.

'Oh, no, no, *no*!' Skye corrected. 'I know exactly the sort of girl he wants. Actually there's a very nice girl working in my section. She saw Warren once when he called to take me to lunch. She called him "a prince"!'

'Don't worry about Warren,' Antonia replied. 'He'll get by.'

Skye had scarcely arrived at the beach for her early morning swim before Jeremy caught up with her. 'Don't go in the water yet, Skye. I have something to say to you.'

'Surely it can't be that urgent?' Skye turned, looking back at him, shading her eyes.

'It *is* urgent.'

It was a brilliant blue day, not a cloud in the sky, and already the board-riders were catching the waves.

'Let's take a walk,' Jeremy, fit and tanned in red and white board shorts, caught hold of Skye's arm.

'Jeremy,' she said gently, 'there's really not much to talk about. I've had a very busy week and I'd like to relax.'

'Reardon's not here.'

'No, he's coming later. There's been some security leak, and Grandfather is furious about it. He's certain it's someone inside the company.'

'Probably.' Jeremy didn't seem too much concerned. 'There's so much security risk in modern business. Photocopiers make it easy for these industrial spies. Then there's so much use of computers. You could shove a tape in your pocket.'

'I know Grandfather's worried,' Skye agreed.

'He never exactly looks worried, does he?' Jeremy remarked with great awe and respect. 'I've never seen such an indomitable old face.'

'He's taking rather a dim view of this business. We probably won't see Guy at all.'

'What a strange relationship you all have,' Jeremy observed. 'Outwardly united, inwardly—who knows?' He lifted his fair head and watched the flight of a seagull. 'Personally I think your grandfather is taking an awful gamble trusting Reardon. They tell me his rise to power has been unprecedented. He's now in an impregnable position, one assumes waiting to take full control when Sir Charles dies.'

'Surely he would have to defeat Uncle Justin first?'

'All he has to do is persuade him to retire gracefully. If it comes to a power struggle Reardon has too much support. I hear a lot of people support him because he's the Reardon heir. Apparently his father was a great bloke—before your grandfather cut him down. Ever think Reardon might be playing you two girls off?'

'I'm sorry, Jeremy, you should draw me pictures,' Skye said quietly.

'Jo Anne thinks he's a man apart.'

'Obviously he *is*.' Skye couldn't prevent herself from saying.

'You're in love with him, aren't you?' Jeremy gave a bitter laugh. 'I knew it at the beginning. You and Jo Anne both. At least Jo Anne has the sense to realise the futility of her chances. She says your grandfather doesn't see anyone but you.'

'Since she doesn't even try to speak to Grandfather!'

Skye exclaimed hotly. 'It takes two to make a relationship work. Grandfather is human. He feels pressured and worried and unhappy. He's attacked by bouts of depression just like you and me. He might look indomitable and to a certain extent he is, but he's vulnerable at some level. Jo Anne doesn't exactly overwhelm him with affection, and God knows she should. He gives her everything, *everything*—too much, yet I've never seen her throw her arms around him or kiss him goodnight, not once.'

'He's not an emotional man.'

'He *is*,' Skye protested in a fine rage. 'He's been a man of strong passions all his life. It's his own family that have never taken the trouble to know him. If there's a breakdown in communications, it's Grandfather's fault. They're too shy, or intimidated, or downright inarticulate to speak their mind. It seems to me they don't want very much to reach him, and they *have* to reach out because he's always been too busy making *them* rich.'

'There's no need to shout!' Jeremy was profoundly shocked at such an outburst. 'For someone who barely knows the man, you understand him all right.'

'Sure I do,' Skye tossed her fiery hair back. 'He's my grandfather—I love him. It's as simple as that.'

'Yet he ignored you all your life?'

'He could ignore me from now on,' Skye said bleakly. 'He's my grandfather. A lot of him is in me.'

'Oh, darling!' Jeremy suddenly reached out and grasped her, bearing her back to the shelter of the sand dunes. 'Kiss me. Please kiss me.'

'Damn it, I won't!'

'Oh, you're an awful bitch!' Jeremy cried in despair, while his mouth made a lunge for hers.

'Oh, Jeremy, don't do this.' Skye was moved to pity.

'It's Reardon's fault. He stole you from me.'

'Why have you got to blame somebody else?' Skye got no further than that, for Jeremy trapped her into

an iron embrace, using his superior strength to force
on her a rough, bitter kiss. She couldn't even struggle
his grip was so strong.

'Darling, darling,' he muttered grindingly against
her mouth.

The only way out of it was to let herself relax, and
Jeremy, encouraged, loosened his ferocious hold.
'You're so beautiful!'

'Jeremy,' she said softly, and used all her strength to
break away from him, 'if you're not going to behave,
you'd better go home, I do *not* love you—I'm sorry.
And it seems to me you weren't half so intent on me
before I was inside the charmed circle. You're very
ambitious and don't deny it.'

'I want you. *Just* you.' Jeremy protested, breathing
heavily.

'No, you don't.' Her glowing eyes stared back at
him defiantly. 'There are some things about me you've
always wanted to change.'

'Well, you are like a miniature volcano,' he said
angrily. 'Too much temperament puts me off.'

'Jo Anne has all the qualities you like.'

'Yes, Jo Anne is very sweet and attractive,' he
agreed strongly. 'I suppose you've been feeling jealous
of her?'

Skye didn't even bother to answer. To Jeremy's
upset and bewilderment, she turned on her heel and
began to run up the beach, an extraordinarily beautiful
sight, hair flying, slender legs covering a surprising
distance. She was wearing a skin-tight one-piece
turquoise bathing suit with a little bit of sleeveless
nothing over it that was now billowing in the wind.
She looked like a dancer performing some new,
ecstatic modern ballet.

Then, quite abruptly, Jeremy turned away. If she
had changed, he was changing himself. It was
certainly flattering to know that Jo Anne was
interested in him. Jo Anne had a lot going for her. She

was rich, she was certainly very glossy and attractive and, the extreme opposite of Skye, she made a man feel ten feet tall. His mother had always said Skye was over-educated, and it certainly looked like it. Clever, quick-tongued women made a man feel threatened. Jeremy plodded out towards the onrushing surf, then when the white foam licked at his ankles, he gathered himself like a charger and ran for the magnificent, translucent cobalt blue arcs under which he could cool his buzzing, confused honey-coloured head.

On the bottom rung of the steps that led up from the beach to the house, Skye poised, breathless. Why ever had she asked Jeremy to come? She hoped he got lost out at sea.

'Well, well, well!' a voice said above her.

She looked up and there stood Guy in all his arrogant, mocking splendour. 'Oh, you've arrived.' She held her hand to the stitch in her side.

'There's a kind of magic in the beach in the mornings, isn't there?' he said conversationally. 'The air is intoxicating.'

'Yes.' She stared at him as he came down the stairs, hands in the pockets of his cotton slacks, the collar of his boldly striped shirt blown up in the breeze. His elegance was stunning, and so was the alertness in his lancing gaze.

'I'm not in the least surprised Jeremy had to cool off,' he commented.

'Ah, you've been spying!'

His quick shudder was quite unfeigned. 'Don't use that word, please!'

'Did you find out something?' she asked.

'Enough to split Maitlands in two.'

'What does that mean?' Skye asked sharply, brushing stray wind-tossed locks out of her eyes.

'Let me think a little more about it before I tell you.'

'Have you told Grandfather?'

Guy stared out over her head at the limitless blue ocean. 'No. When it comes to it, I can't use deliberate cruelty.'

'I see.' She looked down at her narrow feet. 'So you know the name of the villain?'

'I've known for a long time.'

'That's an odd way to put it, Guy.'

'Absolutely.' He brought his gaze back to her again, touching her face, her body, her slender legs. 'What do you think you're doing when my back is turned?'

'Jeremy and I have nothing to do with you.'

'Are you sure?' He took her arm above the elbow, then let his hand slide down to her wrist.

'He's very persistent,' she said shakily. Jeremy's most violent embraces could never elicit this response.

'Yes, he is. Shall I tell him you're meant for me?'

'I don't know. I don't go much for lies.'

'We could work it out so he would believe us,' suggested Guy.

'Don't say a word!' she begged hastily.

'But I don't like it when he allows his mad passions to run rampant. I never realised before, but I have an acutely aggressive streak. If I see him grab you one more time, oblivious to your wishes, his nose may get extended across his face.'

'I can handle it,' she said quietly.

'It didn't look like it.' His silky tone dripped menace. 'For the love of God, he's not drowning himself, is he?'

'Why, what's happening?' Skye spun around in alarm.

'What the hell!' Guy's eyes were trained on Jeremy's bobbing head. Next thing Jeremy's hand came straight up in the air and Guy hurtled across the beach with Skye racing after, no match for his long legs and superior speed.

'He must have a cramp or something!' she shouted.

A board-rider was paddling in fast, but he was too far away, and Jeremy's head had disappeared beneath the foaming silver caps.

Skye's heart accelerated to a rapid rate as she was overcome by remorse. Hadn't she actually wished on Jeremy a watery disaster? 'Oh, what is it?' She raced after Guy furiously. Jeremy was an excellent swimmer. Was it possible he was being pursued by a shark?

Guy, to his eternal credit, didn't even wait to consider. He kicked off his expensive shoes and leapt into the surf, while Jeremy's agonised head popped up again, a mad grimace on his face.

'Are you crazy?' Guy yelled at him, already thinking this was some feckless, rejected lover act,

But Skye was certain Jeremy was in trouble. She recalled just such a face when Jeremy had been struck in the eye by a bouncer at a local cricket match. She dived like a fish under the huge wave that was coming for her, and when she surfaced in the crystal clear trough, Guy's long, powerful silhouette could be seen almost closing on Jeremy. Then there were two heads bobbing in the water, Guy's sleek and black, Jeremy's like a wet collie's.

Eventually Jeremy lay beached on the white sand, gasping pathetically that he had almost drowned.

'We can see that, yes.' Now that he had performed the rescue, Guy was spectacularly annoyed.

'How are you now?' Skye peered down at Jeremy, pressing his shoulder urgently. The board-rider, a tow-haired youth of about seventeen, was on the other side, grinning at Guy as if they were two old friends.

'That's the funniest thing I've ever seen!' he declared.

'You weren't alarmed?' Guy asked him, sleeking back his hair with one hand.

'I was at first. I thought it was a bloody shark. Gee, you're a terrific swimmer, mister—a real iron man!'

'You may well laugh.' Guy glanced down at his soaking wet clothes.

'Make him pay for some new ones,' the youth said. 'Personally I think he was carrying on a bit. What happened, mate, a cramp?'

'They can come on at the most unexpected moments,' Jeremy replied coldly. 'It was agonising while it lasted.'

'You ought to buy a casket ticket to celebrate,' the boy laughed again. 'Come from the big house, do you?'

'Yes,' Skye told him with a nervous glance at Guy.

'What a never-to-be-forgotten morning!' he announced, the first trace of amusement mingled with the scorn.

'Hey, you look a million dollars,' the youth said to Skye. 'I suppose you do modelling?'

'No.'

'You're kidding! You should.'

Guy stood up and offered her his hand. 'All right, Jeremy, or shall we call a cab?'

'Okay, ups-a-daisy!' The youth bent over smilingly and gripped Jeremy's hand. 'I've had cramps myself. At the first sign you should get out of the water.'

'Thank you,' gasped Jeremy. 'You can spare me the lecture!'

The boy turned to Guy and raised his eyebrows wryly. 'Why don't you leave him there next time?'

'I couldn't. There's a long tradition of sea rescue in our family.'

'You don't say.' The boy turned around and picked up his board. 'Well, might see you tomorrow.'

'Just take care of yourself out there,' said Guy.

Jo Anne, when she heard what had happened, couldn't keep calm. 'But how terrible for you, Jeremy!' She went to him, giving him her full attention. 'I think you should lie down.'

'I might for about ten minutes,' Jeremy said. 'It was

quite a severe seizure. Lucky for me Guy was around.'
His colour had returned and his bright hair was
curling all around his head. He looked young and
smooth and in need of mothering. Guy, however,
standing in the doorway, looked too irritated, too
darkly, toughly male, too much a man to be reckoned
with for any such attention.

'Come and rest up,' Jo Anne was saying. 'What
about a couple of aspirin?'

'Can you beat that?' Skye said wonderingly, after
Jeremy was borne away.

'You would ask him, darling,' Guy said gratingly,
'One wonders why.'

'I didn't ask him,' she said shortly. Well, she did ask
him, true, but she didn't want him.

'Then he seems to have a remarkable capacity for
getting in where the ants can't.'

From such an unfortuitous beginning the day
turned out very pleasantly. Jeremy responded to a
good breakfast and once his spirits were up, talked all
the time. They lazed in the sun, swam, went for walks
along the beach and wandered around the shopping
centre, but when Jo Anne suggested a good restaurant
for dinner, Guy drew the line.

'You two go off,' he said in gracious tones. 'Skye
and I will sit at home and enjoy a dull old dinner with
Mother.'

'Wouldn't Mrs Reardon like to come?' Jeremy
suggested to Jo Anne's slight dismay, but Guy told
him briefly that Antonia enjoyed the novelty of
cooking.

As it happened, Skye did the cooking. Antonia had
come to her marriage almost fresh from school and the
question of cooking hadn't really arisen. She had
always lived surrounded by household help, and even
in the apartment she had a cleaning lady and all her
groceries were delivered for her.

'That was splendid!' said Guy with a small sigh, and

stretched his long legs. 'Some man is going to be very proud of you, you know, Skye.'

'As well he should be,' Skye winked at Antonia. 'I'm beautiful, charming, intelligent, I'm a good cook and I love children.'

'You sound perfect.' He glanced up at her, eyes gleaming. 'There's a very romantic moon tonight. We'll get rid of these dishes, then go for a walk.'

'You don't have to stack the dishes at all.' Antonia smiled softly and touched his hand. 'I'll do it.'

'Tonia darling, we wouldn't dream of abandoning you. I know you've never fancied doing the dishes anyway.'

'Oh, how I love this place!' Antonia sighed. 'Remember all our long, lovely holidays together?'

'Of course I do, my love.' Guy picked up his mother's hand and kissed it. 'Which reminds me—let's have Christmas here.'

Looking back at them, Skye felt a tug at her heart. For the first time in her life she had to face this Christmas without her father. She was blinking the tears out of her eyes when Guy came through the door holding a laden tray.

'*Skye*?' There was a look of sudden seriousness on his handsome, relaxed face.

'It won't take us long to put these in the dishwasher.' She looked away quickly, anxious to hide the misting of her eyes.

'Fine.' But he had seen the poignant, haunted look. 'I wonder what Jo and Jeremy are doing now?'

That made her smile. 'Damn it, Guy, don't you care? You're handing over Jo Anne without a struggle!'

'She's certainly developed a sort of wifely attitude towards him. Jo's never really had anyone to fuss over. Some might find it a damned nuisance, but Phillips seems to be at home with that kind of thing. I haven't readily forgotten his mother.'

CHAPTER NINE

IT was quite dark now; half a moon hung in the sky and all the constellations were out—Centaurus lying in the thick diamond daisies of the Milky Way, beside it the Southern Cross, brilliantly defined, nearby Carina with the second brightest star in the sky, Canopus, Orion's belt pointing to the splendour of Sirius. . . .

'Glorious, aren't they?' Skye sighed.

'Superb. They always are at the beach. I like the aboriginal name for the stars, Lilgharlilya for the Milky Way, Jirrunjoonga, the Guiding One, for the Southern Cross. When I was a boy I used to lie on the top balcony and watch them for hours, remembering the old Greek myths about people being banished up there by Zeus; the way the aborigines see the Milky Way as the resting place for their elders.'

'They're so beautiful they make me a little sad,' Skye confessed. 'Beautiful things always made me sad. And intensely happy. Time's passing so quickly, isn't it? None of us have very long.'

'Are you going to come here to me?' Guy asked, a little fiercely. 'The only way any of us are ever going to be happy is to find that one person who fits us exactly.'

'Except they're so terribly difficult to find and sometimes when we find them, it's too late.' They were walking along the edge of the surf, the beautiful ocean breeze coming right at them, silky cool water lapping around their ankles.

'You're melancholy, darling, so early in the evening,' commented Guy.

'Why do you call me darling?' she asked accusingly, and allowed him to take her by a guiding arm.

'To give you a straightforward answer, that's the way I think of you.'

'The word is used so lightly,' she sighed.

'Not by me.' There was no mistaking the arrogance or the certainty of his tone.

'How am I to know?' she asked seriously. 'I think of you as my real friend, yet I know very little about you, Guy. You're almost a stranger.'

'Do you count knowing people in terms of time?'

'I guess I do. For instance, I know everything about Jeremy.'

'Go on.'

'Have you ever been in love, Guy?' she asked.

'Let me see,' he said dryly, 'I've had my heart torn a little. Can you imagine any man who hasn't? When I was about seventeen, I was madly in love all summer.'

'What happened?'

'For the life of me I can't remember. Summer was over and I was off to university. I do remember she was devoted to me—for a while.'

'And nothing serious since?'

'Don't be so silly! I'm thirty-four. I played at love, but getting married has been almost unthinkable. I'd begun to think I wasn't even capable of loving. There was no one woman, however charming, I could bear to settle down with.'

'You sound terribly hard to please,' she observed.

'Yes.' He tightened his arm around her as a little punishment. 'Then one day the woman I want appeared—just like that. She was hellishly unhappy and she didn't even see me. Be *still*!'

But Skye's heart was suddenly hammering in her breast. She knew if she committed herself to Guy there would be no going back. He would never allow it.

'Poor Skye!' he called after her.

Of course there was nowhere to run to, and he caught her easily. 'That's better.' She stood panting, while he clasped her around one wrist. 'Are you frightened I'll make love to you?'

'I think so,' she said fiercely, lifting her hair off her shoulders.

'I'm going to,' he returned quietly, 'in just another minute. What are you frightening, Skye?'

'God knows. A lost cause.'

He dropped both hands to her waist and pulled her into him. 'You spoke about none of us having very much time. I've never been one to waste it. I want you, Skye. I want you so badly, it's almost a pain.'

'Yes, but do you *love* me?'

'I must do.' One of his hands came up under her T-shirt to caress her body. 'Since wherever you go, I follow.'

'I thought you might want me for ... other reasons?' She held up her face to him. 'You want to win so badly, don't you, Guy?'

'I just don't want to, my love, I'm *going* to.' The thrilling, vibrant tones had gone hard. 'But that doesn't mean to say you should see yourself as a pawn in the game. I'd want you,' he said coolly, 'if I'd only seen you in a passing car. I don't give a damn that you're a Maitland.'

She drew back against his insistent hand. 'You're angry.'

'All right, I'm angry. The damned fool ideas you get in your head!'

'Surely you don't think ideas can't touch me?' Her face was upflung, flushed with the sudden heat of excitement, her breeze-tossed hair a curling cloud around her, eyes flashing in the silver gloom.

'No talk,' Guy said harshly, getting his arms around her. 'I don't want to *talk*.'

Skye cried out when he lifted her, but he was shockingly strong. There was nothing else to do but cling to him, her arms locked around his neck. Desperately she tried to hold on to her whirling senses, but they were being blown away from her, scattering on the wind. He had no right to dominate her so easily. No right at all.

Guy must have already decided on the exact place, for he carried her to a sheltered spot where the sand was covered in soft vegetation and in the sunlight, flat, golden flowers.

'Guy?'

'What is it?' His voice was low and urgent.

'You don't know?' How could he *not* know she was frightened?

'I won't hurt you,' he said. 'I'd never hurt you. I have a million things I can do to you before that.'

Desire raged through every fibre of her body, obliterating panic. Even the cooling sea breeze couldn't bank down the fire in her blood. In contrast to the tangy darkness that surrounded them, brain and body seemed pierced with light. Whatever the bond between them, it was very, very strong and very, very, special.

With Guy poised over her, her whole body trembled in readiness. His mouth was only inches away and she reached up a hand and curled it around his nape. '*Please*,' she murmured, protesting his deliberate torment.

He seemed to sigh as though he needed that soft, whispered entreaty, then his open mouth came down over hers, at first gently, then with increasing intensity.

It was like drowning in a sea of sensuality, and when he lifted his head briefly, Skye heard herself moan. He was lifting her a little, undoing the catch of her flimsy net bra, then she lay perfectly still in anticipated shock as his hands sought and caressed the swelling mounds of her breasts.

The pleasure was so intense that her body jerked in ecstasy, then his mouth took over from his hands, his lips closing over the hard, flushed peaks of her breasts.

'*Guy!*' Did she whisper his name, or was it a moan deep inside her?

'This is *hell*!' he muttered in a driven voice. 'Heaven. Quite, quite mad to make love to you here.'

Skye didn't answer—couldn't, as his hand trailed down over her body, spearing beneath the white cotton jeans she was wearing, across the silky skin of her stomach to the secret core of her body.

'I want you,' he was saying. '*God!*'

She thought she would go mad with excitement and longing. It was like ceding control of her own body to a radiant power she was wise enough to fear.

'We can't stay here, darling,' Guy said bluntly. 'We both know what will happen.'

She had to shake her head to clear it. 'All right,' she said shakily, but she lacked the strength to move.

'For the love of God,' he groaned, his head pressed into her scented shoulder. 'It's incredible what power you wield!'

'You see?' she whispered, and turned her throbbing mouth against the silken rasp of his cheek. 'You resent me.'

'I'll show you resentment!' He kissed her, caressed her again with such mastery that she burst into tears. 'Oh, darling, *don't*!'

'What are we going to *do*, Guy?' she wept.

He stared down at her, her face a pale flower in the glimmering darkness. 'What was inevitable from the moment I saw you. I made my choice then.'

'You could have told me!' Her sharp, inward breath was a gasp.

'I thought I'd give you a little time. Your skin is like silk,' he said as he licked up her tears. 'Is it possible I *could* have you, all to myself?'

'What are you asking?' Tremulously she dropped her hand over the one cupped so possessively around her breast.

'Dates, I guess. If I actually picked you up and

carried you out of your room tonight, could I make you pregnant?'

'Would you want to?' she whispered.

'Yes.' He lifted her chin and kissed her mouth. 'Very definitely yes. About three times. But I don't care much for right now. We need time to ourselves for a while. At the very least, a whole year.'

'Do you mean you want to get *married*?' The shock was so much, her tears had stopped.

'Or nothing,' he said briskly. 'If you think you're making a fool out of me, you've got another think coming.'

'But so *fast*!'

'All right. I'll give you six months, but I want to bring you to my bed.'

'I don't know, Guy,' she said in response to her inner panic. 'It's like a dream.'

'I didn't dare to believe in it either, but not only do I worship the way you look, the whole spirit of you touches me even more deeply. I have to discover everything about you.'

'Can you hear my heart pounding?' she asked faintly.

He moved slowly, lowering his head until it rested against her heart. 'Marvellous!' he moaned. 'The object of my passion is a devastatingly shy and innocent little virgin!'

'Did you want someone with more experience?' she asked.

'No.' He moved his thumb back and forth over her taut nipple. 'It's obvious your potential is quite enormous. Now, have you calculated when I can make love to you?'

'Endlessly,' she wavered. 'Though I think I'd be disgusted with myself if I allowed you to seduce me in your mother's beach house.'

'Then we'd better go home.' He pulled her to him and rocked them both gently.

'Guy,' Skye murmured in a crazed little voice. She couldn't withhold herself much longer. Now now when she was going molten.

'All right,' he hissed against her ear. 'Sleep in your own bed and I'll make love to you by remote control. You'll wake up and imagine there's someone beside you, someone planting kisses all over your beautiful body. You'll be wearing nothing. For that matter, neither will I.'

'Torturer!' She dipped her head and sighed into his throat. She had never felt so delirious in her life.

All the following week, Sir Charles looked feverishly preoccupied, tired and old. The news of an important security leak had spread like flames not only through the companies but the city's financial heart. Details of a proposed fifty-million-dollar project had been handed to a competitor, and although the theft couldn't entirely wreck the project the identity of the thief had become a terrible headache. Skye, so close to her grandfather now, could feel his feverish concern. Uncle Justin with his cold hostility towards Guy had pointed out his easy access to all of Maitland's most vital secrets, but Sir Charles had shrugged that off with a terrible gleam in his eyes.

'Guy would be the last person to move in such a fashion,' he had laughed bleakly. 'I have my own suspicions, but I simply can't give them a name.'

Warren, too, seemed terribly burdened. 'If Guy had anything to do with it,' he told his cousin, 'Grandfather will find it out. Dad claims that Guy has been given incredible power in the last two years. I've seen him myself with all the high security files.'

'Why ever would he want to wreck a project he himself was responsible for?' Skye found herself answering with more than a suggestion of anger in her voice. 'It seems to me Uncle Justin is spreading these rumours about Guy.'

'Why do you say that?' Warren's dark eyes had opened in disbelief. 'You know nothing about the company, Skye. Dad has always said Guy is only waiting his chance to destroy us.'

'Only I'm convinced he wouldn't work in such an underhand way.'

'But then again, it makes a kind of sense. . . .'

Whoever had done it, Skye thought bleakly, was playing a dangerous game. The situation in the household was fasting becoming unnerving, the affair every bit as noxious to her as it was to her grandfather. No investigators had been called in, but meanwhile Guy, so far as Justin Maitland was concerned, was under suspicion. God knows what possessed him to do it, Justin argued privately, except a good deal of money.

Skye thought about it all endlessly. There was no question Guy was all-absorbed in winning back his father's empire. And more. Yet he was a strong man—bold, far stronger and bolder than Uncle Justin, who was all but calling on Guy's letter of resignation. Guy, to everyone's eyes, was totally secure within himself, sure of his ability, ambitions and manipulative skills. The theft seemed wholly inconsistent with his style.

For Skye it was a very long week indeed—draining. If Guy was any way implicated in the theft! It was unthinkable. She listened, angry and agonised, as Uncle Justin told them over the dinner table, 'it all fitted'. Every time anyone went to contradict him or to speak he glared so wildly, it was a further embarrassment. Only Sir Charles and Guy kept their own counsel.

Skye had lunch with Antonia, neither of them broaching the subject until almost the end of the meal.

'Guy knows who it is,' said Antonia.

'Then why doesn't he *say*?' Skye asked urgently.

'I'm sure he will.' Antonia's large, shining eyes were full of a curious light. 'Whoever photocopied those documents was a reckless and foolish man. Careless, too, Guy told me.'

Skye found her grandfather one night, head down, thumb and finger pressed to his tired eyes.

'This is upsetting you dreadfully, isn't it, Granddad?' she asked him, perched as usual on the side of his huge, bronze-studded leather chair. 'There's something more to this than an industrial theft?'

'You know your uncle Justin has been maligning Guy?'

'It *can't* be Guy,' she said throbbingly.

'It didn't take long for him to win you,' Sir Charles said, a little sadly.

'But, Granddad. . . .' She was flustered that she seemed so transparent.

'No buts.' Sir Charles patted her hand. 'You're in love with him, aren't you? I've known from the beginning how he felt about you. He was ready to love you before he ever met you. Pre-destined, I suppose. I didn't believe much in that sort of stuff, yet I see it happening before my eyes. It couldn't be coincidence that Guy's father took Tonia off my boy.'

Skye glanced down at her grandfather, marvelling at the revelation. 'Off Uncle Justin, you mean?'

'Indeed he did. I'm surprised you haven't heard that before. Justin went into his shell then and has never come out since. I don't think you realise what a handsome man he was. Much less fascinating than Reardon, of course. I suppose, compared to him, dull, but he did love Tonia.'

'I never knew.'

'Well, you're not the only one,' Sir Charles patted her hand. 'I've a few things left to learn. All of us have been punished in our own way. You seem to be the only one who escaped the bitterness.'

The following night Guy arrived at the house and they all knew, immediately they set eyes on him, that something was wrong. His entrance, dark, unsmiling, diamond-hard, seemed to be calculated to strike fear into the collective Maitland heart.

'Guy, what's wrong?' Felicity went quickly to him, laying an almost beseeching hand on his arm.

'It would be better if Sir Charles explained the results of our meeting to you,' he answered with remote courtesy. He lifted his head and saw Skye poised on the staircase, so apprehensive she felt unable to descend. His silver eyes were glittering, but he never said a word. He was still dressed in his sombre, elegant city clothes and he carried a black briefcase bulging out of its smooth line.

'Ah, there you are, Guy,' Sir Charles, unnoticed, had emerged from his study.

'Good evening, sir.'

Sir Charles looked at him, looked at the briefcase and turned about. 'Come along, then, let's get it over. God help anyone up against you!'

Felicity seemed to have stiffened into a statue, and Skye went to her. 'Are you all right, Aunt Felicity?'

For once Felicity didn't correct her. She turned to Skye with tears in her eyes. 'You realise what this means?'

'No.' Skye shook her head.

'It means Guy is going to crucify someone.'

'He couldn't be that cruel.' Skye led an unresisting Felicity back into the drawing room. 'You're frightened about something, aren't you?'

Felicity didn't draw away, she moved closer, seemingly comforted by Skye's young presence. 'Oh God, Skye, what are we going to do?'

'It's Uncle Justin you're worried about, isn't it?' Skye said quietly.

'Where is he now?' Felicity's clear, confident voice had a tremor in it.

'He's a busy man.'

'You know that's not it, dear.'

'No.'

'I've thought for a long time that Justin was heading for disaster. Do you know anything about your uncle Justin and Guy's mother?'

Skye bit her lip. 'Granddad said something the other night.'

'He loved her madly.' Felicity's thin face crumpled. 'Of course it had to end tragically. I suppose it will all come out.'

'What will?' Skye had to swallow over the painful lump in her throat.

'Jealousy destroys people, Skye, you know. Or maybe you will never know. You have such beautiful qualities, a great capacity for forgiveness. It's not a Maitland trait.'

Skye took Felicity's hand and held it. 'Are you trying to tell me that you think Uncle Justin is implicated in this theft?'

'I'm sure Guy isn't,' Felicity returned grimly. 'Guy can do everything he has to do legitimately. He's a high-tech wizard and there's no limit on what he can do. His micro-chip designs are earning us a fortune, and better than that, what he's working on now will benefit mankind. Our medical advances are world-famous, as you know. No, Guy, doesn't have to stoop to treachery. What was it Milton said about the devil?'

'That it was better to reign in Hell than serve in Heaven?'

'I'm certain,' Felicity said tonelessly, 'that Justin schemed and informed and lied to bring Julian down. For years the rumours have put the blame on Grandfather, but generally speaking Grandfather fights fair. No one could claim he's not ruthless in his way, but I don't believe he was responsible for Julian's ruin.'

'And who was, my dear, eh? Who was?'

Both women turned as Justin Maitland came

towards them, his tall, lean figure outlined in a beam of light.

'Oh, Justin, you're home,' Felicity murmured, going so pale Skye tightened her grip on Felicity's hand.

'Tell us more,' Justin invited, not sitting down but pouring himself a drink.

'Guy is here,' she said baldly.

'So?'

'So what is he here *for*?'

'Possibly to hand in his resignation.'

Felicity blinked, unsure of herself again. 'I don't think so, dear.'

'My life story,' Justin said dryly, 'having to dispose of the Reardons.'

'Even to destroying them?' Skye asked gravely.

Her uncle turned and gave her a frowning grimace. 'Why don't you mind your own business, young lady?'

'This *is* my business.'

'I see, and how is that?'

'Guy has asked me to marry him.'

Felicity didn't look in the least surprised, but Justin sat down in an armchair and shouted with bitter laughter. 'How incredible!'

'So I'm on Guy's side,' she explained.

'Of course.' Justin Maitland nodded his complete acceptance. 'The Reardon men have taken a heavy toll of our women.'

'*I'm* your wife, Justin,' Felicity said bleakly.

'Fine,' Justin shrugged. 'I doubt whether that crosses your mind when you're having your affairs.'

'No affairs, Justin, I swear. Meaningless little diversions to make me feel like a woman. You've never had *me* on your mind.'

At that moment a very unhappy-looking Warren confronted them. 'Dad,' he said with some difficulty, 'you're wanted in the study.'

Justin Maitland said nothing. He stood up, threw

off his drink, repositioned his tie, then stalked out of the room.

Behind him, Felicity started to cry.

Warren paused for a moment, obviously under a great strain. 'This is bad, Mamma, you understand?'

'But it's all in the family!' Skye had to answer, Felicity was so distressed. 'Can't we settle whatever it is among ourselves?'

'I don't think we can, because Guy won't let us.'

'Oh God!' Skye sat powerless, visualising Guy's forbidding demeanour. The Reardon turn had come and there was no question that all the Reardons were extremely bitter.

'You're the only one who could get to him,' Warren said with a flush of colour in his cheeks. 'You're the only Maitland he cares for. He'd destroy the rest of us in moments. I swear to you I know Guy can be ruthless. He thinks his father is dead because of us.'

'You're not to blame, are you?' said Skye. 'You wouldn't hurt a fly. Your mother certainly isn't, neither is Jo Anne. You're the innocent bystanders. You can't be expected to pay the price.'

'Think about it, Skye,' Warren begged. 'You saw Guy when he came in. He'd execute his best friend if he found him in the wrong.'

'You don't know Guy,' she shook her head. 'There must be a way around this. There's *got* to be.'

'Either way, Dad's finished,' Warren said flatly.

An hour later Guy came out of the study, his striking face chiselled in stone. It appeared he wasn't going to speak to anyone, and Skye flew after him, catching him at the door. 'Weren't you even going to speak to me?'

'Or another way of putting it, weren't you going to speak to *me*?'

'But you look so unapproachable.'

'That's how I feel,' he said coldly.

'Can't I come with you, *please*?' Skye begged.

'You realise what I've done?'

'Yes.'

His silver eyes were stirred into a dark grey storm. 'You must want something, Skye?' He spoke so icily she dropped her entreating arm.

'I'm a Maitland to you now, is that it?' She looked up at him now with undisguised hostility.

'I know you've got a lot of the old man in you. Probably you're going to do a deal with me?'

'I could slap your face!' she said angrily.

'Then you'd be a fool.' He lifted his hand to her nape and clenched his hand around it. 'You might be a Maitland, but you're their finest example.'

'I'm coming with you, Guy,' she said passionately.

'You might be sorry.' There was a prowling darkness somewhere inside him.

'That's my problem.'

He stood back and bowed ironically. 'Step into my parlour, said the spider to the fly.'

'Where *are* we going?' she was forced to ask him in the car. He was driving too fast, taking absolutely no notice of her.

'My place. Surely you understood that?'

'Can't we go somewhere else? Antonia's?'

'No, we can't,' he said briefly. 'Do you want to get out?'

'It's Uncle Justin, isn't it?' she asked in a doomed voice.

'Betrayal is the worst sin, violet eyes. It simply doesn't do to betray one's own father, let alone a man one only considers has wronged one.'

'How would *you* feel about a man who took *me*?'

'I'd tell you after I killed him.'

'So there?'

'Please, darling,' he said jeeringly, 'I'm talking with my feelings. A man has to take it straight. My mother never loved Justin Maitland. She believed she cared for him—for a short time. Much as you cared for

Jeremy, who seems bent on joining the family one way or the other. Don't try to soften me up—I won't listen. I've fixed that bastard for good. Something I've been working on for the past five years.'

'You mean . . . ?'

'He hanged himself,' he chopped her off savagely.

'Am I allowed a final question?'

'No.'

They finished the rest of the trip in silence, and Skye thought with despair that she could never rescue him from his course of vengeance. If indeed she had the right to. Where were her uncle's morals? He had played the role of betrayer, not once, but twice.

Soft downlights bathed Guy's apartment in a sea of light. Like Antonia's it had a splendid view of the harbour and the city's lights. It had tremendous impact too, the subdued and refined design a wonderful foil for the art works, both paintings and sculpture, but this wasn't the time to concentrate on either.

'Come in,' Guy invited her mockingly. 'There's no need to be overly timid.'

'I'm not timid at all.'

He laughed. 'No, you're not. What are you here for, Skye?'

She turned and looked at him. 'Because I want to be here with you. Because I want to know what's going on. Because I care about my grandfather—and all the rest of them, for that matter. But most of all, because I care about *you*.'

'Thank you, darling. That was a magnificent little speech.' Guy walked to a sliding glass door and opened it to the balcony overlooking the harbour. The night was black and starry, and all around them millions of lights burned, red, green, gold, electric blue, like a limitless jewel-box.

'It wasn't a speech,' Skye told him, 'it was words from my heart.'

'I see—your heart. And what *is* the state of your heart? No matter whatever I was hoping I've never heard you say you love me.'

'But *you* have never said you love *me*.' She didn't say it accusingly, but gently.

'Come here to me,' he said.

She looked at his face, cast in a ruthless, passionate, mould. 'I do love you,' she said, very simply and directly.

'Handy to say it now.'

'Do you want to hear it again?' She went to him, aware that he was standing very, very still. Odd to think he looked enormously powerful and threatening.

'Yes.' He didn't touch her.

'I love you, Guy.'

'You mean you'll marry me whenever I want?'

'Yes,' she said breathlessly, 'but shouldn't we talk things out?'

'What things?' He put his hands around her face—not gently.

'You're very upset, aren't you?' she said quietly.

'No, darling,' he said very bitterly. 'I'm happy with what I've done. I want you to know it. Maybe you won't be so wrapped up in your new-found love.'

'I believe you want to hurt *me*?' she said in a curious voice, her heart thudding in slow, painful strokes.

'Hurt you?' His hand slid into her hair, grasped a handful. 'I've been waiting for you all my life!'

'I understand, Guy,' she said urgently.

'*Do* you?' Underneath the harshness was a note that she knew. His eyes dropped to her mouth, not hard or remote, but lit by small flames.

'Yes.' Her eyes were full of tears, a blazing blue-violet. 'If Uncle Justin has plunged off the beaten track, don't let's follow him. Let Grandfather settle him. He'll do it, you know—you must know that.'

Guy brought his mouth down on hers, very urgently, then withdrew it.

'*Oh!*' Her eyes flickered as she lost him. Involuntarily she clutched at him, the seeming rebuff too much for her, but he lifted her and carried her shivering into the pearl-grey bedroom.

She fell on to the lustrous fitted bedspread and rolled away towards a wall lined with beautifully framed architectural drawings, her mind dancing with shock.

And so here it is, she thought. She couldn't stop him. She didn't want to. She had been lost to him on sight.

Guy took her gently by the shoulder and drew her back to him. 'Even if this doesn't solve anything, I need you—too badly.'

'I love you. I'll be with you no matter what happens,' she said.

'Hush!' He spoke to her as if to a child, but it was a woman's body he bared to his hands. 'You're so beautiful,' he said. 'So beautiful, I can't think.'

His touch was electric, arching her yearning body.

'I love you,' she whispered, and pressed her mouth against his shoulder.

'Stay with me tonight.' He held her to him. 'I can't do without you another night of my life.'

'I can't.' Skye put back her head so he could kiss her throat. 'There's Granddad.'

'Let him fight his own battles.'

'He's old now, Guy. Ready to break.'

'He let his son try to break *me*.'

'No,' Skye shook her head. 'He always knew who would win in the end. Just as he knows who will take over when he dies.' The tips of her fingers were massaging his neck, unlocking the tension. 'I'm going to spend all my life with you. I *have* to go home tonight.'

'What if I don't let you out?' His hands came down over her young, sculptured breasts.

'Can you feel my heart beating?'

'Out of control.' His mouth roamed all over her face, prolonging the moment until he reached her mouth.

'Tell me you'll leave this to Granddad,' she begged him.

'Who's controlling who around here?' Guy lowered her back against the bolster, her hair like flame against the pearl-grey lustre.

'You have the whip hand, Guy. You know it. You feel it. You're not cruel.'

'I am—you've no idea.' He allowed his hands to shape her body.

'Look at me,' she begged.

'I'm afraid I might drown in your eyes.'

'Let's start the Reardons and the Maitlands all over again. Let's do it the right way. There'll be no one to stand between us. Granddad will arrange it. You don't need me to tell you that.'

'When I think of that bastard!' Guy gave a great, shuddering sigh.

'You've dealt with it.'

'I know.' He looked into her eyes for a long moment.

'Let Granddad clean up the mess, as befitting his position. He *is* Maitlands and he *is* Uncle Justin's father.'

'He's not appreciating that at the moment,' Guy said wryly. 'All right, if I'm going to do *you* one almighty favour, can I continue undressing you?'

'Any time,' Skye put up her arms and drew him down to her, 'after we're married.'

'Wait a minute.' He turned his head and bit her ear gently.

'You heard.'

'My God, I can't *stand* it!' he muttered.

'Yes, you can.'

'I *can't*.' He drew her towards him, almost crushing her to prove the point.

'It's only going to be a few weeks.'

'Don't fool with me, Skye,' he warned her.

'I mean it. My solemn promise. Besides, I can't stand it either.'

'Damn,' he breathed, yet the lines of tension were completely erased. 'What kind of blackmail is this?'

Her brilliant eyes looked at him, shining with love. 'Think of our wedding night.'

'What did you say?' Miraculously he smiled, as pure happiness got the better of bitterness forever.

'I said,' she leaned forward, punctuating her words with kisses, 'just ... think ... of ... our ... wedding ... night!'

Whatever he decided, she was going to do.

'Little girl,' he groaned, 'you don't know what you're asking. You're in my veins like a life's blood.'

'So what about our wedding night?' she asked softly.

'Mm.' Guy leaned his dark head back and closed his eyes. 'I think I'll make love to you until you're unconscious.'

'Best I know what's going on, though, don't you think?' Skye hung above him, then bent and kissed his mouth, unable in this last minute to stop. It wasn't easy to talk about banking the fires when radiance was shooting through her like quicksilver.

'Stop that!' He flipped her over and held her down quivering. 'How can you possibly expect me to behave when I'm scorching up?'

'Oh, Guy, I love you,' she said, and stroked the side of his cheek. 'Let's go and tell Tonia.'

Begin a long love affair with

HARLEQUIN SUPERROMANCE.™

Accept LOVE BEYOND DESIRE **FREE.**

Complete and mail the coupon below today!

- -